Like a Wary Blessing

Michael Jennings

A Wings ePress, Inc.
Short Story Collection

Wings ePress, Inc.

Edited by: Jeanne Smith
Copy Edited by: Brian Hatfield
Executive Editor: Jeanne Smith
Cover Artist: Trisha FitzGerald-Jung

All rights reserved

Names, characters and incidents depicted in this book are products of the author's imagination or are used fictitiously. Any resemblance to actual events, locales, organizations, or persons, living or dead, is entirely coincidental and beyond the intent of the author or the publisher.

No part of this book may be reproduced or transmitted in any form or by any means, electronic or mechanical, including photocopying, recording, or by any information storage and retrieval system, without permission in writing from the publisher.

Wings ePress Books
www.wingsepress.com

Copyright © 2021 by: Michael Jennings
ISBN 978-1-61309-549-2

Published In the United States Of America

Wings ePress Inc.
3000 N. Rock Road
Newton, KS 67114

What They Are Saying About

Like a Wary Blessing

Michael Jennings's collection of short stories takes readers on thought-provoking journeys in search for meaning from traumatic events and experiences. His tormented characters try to come to terms with the reality of senseless deaths during the Vietnam War, confronting racial tensions in Army boot camp, trying to find joy in a material world, and other dark encounters. Jennings is especially effective in revealing their innermost feelings while presenting keenly descriptive scenes.
— Michael Embry, author of John Ross Boomer Lit series

A hard-hitting collection of short stories that transports the reader from the vibrant jungles of Vietnam to the parched heart of the Arabian Desert, Michael Jennings's latest works reveal the anguish, pain, and loneliness of men separated from those they love. Jennings's words are fresh, unique and memorable—just curl your tongue around "the brittle lip of the desert night," and shift your vision to "eyes that gleam like knobs of bone."

Jennings's stories will linger in your memory long after reading, and you will never be quite the same person you were before you read them. Highly recommended!
—Chris Helvey, author of Violets for Sergeant Schiller

Dedication

Dedicated to the memory of Joseph Allen Horne, Jr.

* * *

Table of Contents

Night Mission 1

Cadence Count 16

Papa-san's Private War 69

A Valley of Dead Marines 81

The Inland Sea 110

Harry and the Ugly Rug 137

Dawn Call 145

Night Mission

All that dry season, I lived in a two-man cubicle with a big, swart Italian in whose face a cigar seemed a healthily obscene anatomical part. Buonacone and I worked a twelve-hour shift in an aerial reconnaissance shop by the flight line. We sat on tall dunce stools and hunched over tables that had fluorescent bulbs beneath their glass surfaces and reels at either end. Across our light tables we cranked infrared film splotched with the ghosts of troop formations and trucks and equipment-laden water buffalo and elephants moving in darkness down the Ho Chi Minh Trail.

You knew you weren't seeing the men or machines or beasts moving beneath the jungle canopy, but only the heat they emitted. Yet as you gazed at these images through your stereo viewer, there grew upon you the conviction that you alone saw their essence, their life. You felt it was daylight photography, dependent as vision depends on merely reflected light, that was superficial. You knew that, however dark the night, however dense the foliage, life's emanation betrays it to those who possess the proper emulsion. Reeling the film across the tables, plugging the altitude and angle of obliquity into the formulas that yielded dimensions, you felt gifted with preternatural cunning.

As our sweat dripped onto the film in our sweltering trailer by the flight line, we would sometimes stand upright, cursing and rubbing our eyes, trying to decide whether to call a cluster of blobs one hundred probable troops or four probable elephants. But as the weather grew drier and hotter, more often the nighttime traffic along the Trail gave us a feeling of overabundance.

Twice each shift, Sergeant Baptiste clomped into our trailer to collect the reports we filled out in block lettering. He would take them off to be transmitted by secure Teletype to targeting teams at all four in-country air bases that sent daylight bombing missions over the Trail. He told us word was filtering back that the F-100 pilots who used our work often climbed down from their cockpits looking sheepish when they'd finished their missions. He said they felt as if they'd merely plinked plastic ducks that floated out into their field of fire precisely when we'd predicted. We'd stripped them of what they valued most in their job, its risk and uncertainty.

We would get back to our cubicle in the barracks at dawn and stay in bed until the heat and the screeching of jet afterburners and the blaring stereos and the maids' gabbling drove us out before noon. We found that putting on life jackets and floppy jungle hats and sunglasses and lying submerged to the ears in the big, elevated concrete swimming pool behind the base library was a fair anodyne for grating sleeplessness.

In the mornings, Thi-Thi would move swiftly through the barracks with her splayed bare feet thumping heel-first on the floor. Her smile had a dimpled softness that set it apart from the pro forma smiles the other maids wore. I could not attach a name to what I felt when she swung past, carrying her big feather duster, her round face shining, her black hair in an arched ponytail jouncing. Nameless too was the thrill, like the spasm of a strange, deep muscle, when I heard her pant. She was always softly panting.

There was a rule against putting up plywood partitions in the barracks. Our NCOs told us to nail them up anyway, leaving a central fire corridor, and paint them and present the Marine Corps with a *fait accompli*. Once we'd built our cubicle and Thi-Thi had to venture into our lair to clean, I began to attack her in playful earnest.

"Oh, oh, oh, Thi-Thi, he's gotcha now!" Buonacone would boom when I leapt from my pretended doze toward the sound of her panting and grabbed her ankle or wrist, as she dusted or collected our boots for polishing. "Oh, oh, I would say that somebody stands in danger of severe and repeated violation, Thi-Thi!" As we tussled, Buonacone would re-light the cigar he had left at dawn in the pewter ashtray, shaped like a baseball home plate, atop his footlocker. With his laughter, he would bellow forth the foul fumes of twice-smoked tobacco.

Her smile would widen and her panting would quicken and she would battle me nimbly and well. She would brace a foot or a hand against the bed frame and I couldn't budge her. She would swat me in the face with her feather duster until, blinded and choking, I let her go. Buonacone would grasp his knees and rock back on his bed with glee.

"That's dousin' him, Thi-Thi!" he would roar around his erected cigar. "That's showin' him the li-bi-di-nal lamp is *out*!"

Buonacone was from Jersey City, and he had played catcher and batted cleanup for a college in Connecticut. In his generous wop heart, he harbored the delusion that his teammates could win without him. The scores of college games would come in about noon at the AFN station on the Army base next door, but only the scores of big-name schools would get announced on air. On days when Buonacone expected results for a Braddock College game, he'd cram a pocket with cigars to pass out to the station crew in case the spirits of Ruth and Keeler had visited a crypt-like New England dugout. Then he would saunter forth, rocking upward on the balls of his feet, trailing the pungent blue incense of masculine hope.

One morning, after Buonacone ambled off toward the AFN station, chanting a staccato ditty around his teeth-clenched cigar, Thi-Thi thumped into the cubicle and pulled my big toe so hard it loudly popped.

"Hoi!" she said with a beautiful smile. Then she popped the other big toe and said "Ha!" Next, she went through a dumb show of dusting Buonacone's footlocker while edging an ankle toward me and gleaming at me out of the corner of an eye.

I can't call the edging forth of the ankle and the gleam either brazen or coy, for they didn't register on the glib, daylight emulsion that our work had caused to go stale. What did register was her quick panting. It seemed a breathy echo of our night-times, of the secret emanations from men and beasts of burden, from radiant metal and crouching jungle predators.

I grabbed the tiny ankle beneath the black pajama leg. She hopped on the unsnared foot to my bed, and sat with the fingers of one hand pressed lightly against my chest.

"Hey—hey—you buy me PX," she panted.

I wasn't disappointed. I had no thought of sleeping with her. She had told me she had a husband in the infantry somewhere, and a child. If I had to be rear echelon, I didn't care to be that kind of rear echelon. What excited me was not her beauty or her possible willingness, but the dark, faltering emanation from her breast.

"Tell me what you want. Baby food?" Because the Army PX humanely stocked it, for the men who kept mistresses.

"Yes, beh-by," she nodded. "For beh-by. You buy me cig'rette." She took her fingers from my chest and unfolded the piaster bills she'd held crumpled in the other palm. The crinkling sound the notes made resembled the clacking of Teletype keys, and as I took them, I pictured Buonacone, wrapped in a poisonous cloud, leaning above the machine, scanning the baseball scores and stats.

Each week I bought her a carton of cigarettes, which she sold, probably at triple profit, on the black market. I would have given her all the food she wanted, but the one time I gave her jars of baby food she grew so abashed that I decided her way was better. What she wanted as much as baby food was the chance to add value through her own enterprise. I settled for pretending the cigarettes cost less than they did, though not so much less that she'd suspect my charity.

During that long dry season, I wrote to my ordinary daylight images of two women, images that had to do with the one's holding a tough news job and the other's being much sought after. I wrote to them in good faith, but their images remained less real to me than the dark, guttering flame in Thi-Thi's breast that made her pant that way.

After the rains set in and traffic on the Trail dwindled to nearly nothing, Buonacone and I got our commendation medals. The colonel said our work for the past half year matched up well with what men in our job and pay grade had done during the missile crisis, when they'd spotted launch sites the Cubans and Russians had shrouded with leaves and netting. We didn't exactly pop our chests out when the colonel pinned on our ribbons, but for about a day and a half, we didn't feel too bad about it either.

"Congratu-laaa-tions!" Sergeant Baptiste said the next night when he clomped up the short flight of steps into our two-man shop. His gleaming rack of teeth outshone our light tables.

Since the rains started, the tables' fluorescent glow had served only to illuminate the pointlessness of our being there at all. Our pilots had quit running infrared missions. We'd gotten no film for weeks. Each night we'd go to the shop and shoot paper clips at the geckos that scampered across the outside of our window screens. It's tough spooking a gecko enough to make him tumble off a screen, but you can do it if it's a big clip and it hits right below his chin.

At least we could kill time in some comfort. Once our daily deliveries of film stopped, Buonacone scrounged two swivel chairs with backrests from the AFN station, so we wouldn't have to perch hour after hour on the dunce stools like parrots in a cage. When we'd been on call six hours, Sergeant Baptiste would clomp up the steps and tell us we could go.

The night after we got the medals, though, he'd appeared just halfway into our on-call shift, and he'd brought a reel of film. He said it was a few weeks old and it had already made the rounds of F-100 squadrons.

"Lookee, lookee!" he said, waggling the metal film canister at us like a stripteaser waggling her loins. "Nobody north of the DMZ knows it, but you two probably account for more gook soldiers getting blown ass over pith helmet than all B-52 missions flown since Christ was a cadet. Difference is, none of those bomber crews has a clue what's down there in sectors they carpet-bomb. You guys tell pilots exactly where to hunt the live meat."

He gave the film canister another coy little waggle. "Little mama-sans with their dinky little shovels very much included," he said. "We've got aerial *and* ground-level intel that shows enough of 'em are getting blown sky-high to make it rain pink."

Buanocone was leaning back in his chair, poised to fire a paperclip. For a while he stayed frozen in ready-aim position. Then he slowly lowered the unfired paperclip and turned his swivel chair with a couple of toe-taps.

"Hey Sarge, you always say we're your favorite turds, right?" he said.

Sergeant Baptiste opened the film canister. "That's rii-ight," he said soothingly. "Two absolutely primo-grade turds. I'd never shit you."

He fitted the full reel onto a spindle at one end of my light table and unspooled enough film to span the table's radiant surface. He slotted the film's free end in the take-up reel and punched the scroll button. It was daylight photography, shot at low enough altitude to make anything taller than a buffalo's newborn calf pop into three dimensions when viewed through a stereoscope. Baptiste nudged the stereo viewer on its spindly wire legs to a spot on the film that was circled with a black grease pencil.

"That stack there is mostly little mama-sans," Baptiste said, tapping a finger on the film. "Look close and you can see their dinky little shovels."

Through the viewer I could see the pile of corpses. From its shadow length, I judged it was about five feet tall. On its top tier I could make out little white feet below black pajama legs. Shovels and conical hats were strewn around the bodies like paint chips left by a sloppy house painter who'd hurried off to happy hour.

Baptiste said 16- and 17-year-old girls volunteered to come down from the North to make overnight road repairs. When a convoy was headed south, the girls would often march a day ahead of it, he said.

That way they could repair bomb damage in time for vehicles to roll right through. He said the CIA had human assets in Laos who'd heard the girls laughing and singing as they marched past.

"Waste of a lot of mousy little poontang, you ask me," Baptiste said, shaking his head. "But, hey. It wasn't like you and me were about to get any of that anyway, was it?"

Buonacone pushed himself up from the swivel chair with enough force to propel it backward against the trailer wall. He swatted me aside with an arm, then bent to look through my stereo viewer.

"Next convoy must've pulled over long enough to stack 'em up like that," Baptiste said. "Just to get them out of the way, you know."

"And you said you'd never shit us," Buonacone said, still gazing through the viewer. His voice was just a raspy whisper. Then he stood upright and squinted at Sergeant Baptiste.

"So how come you never told us?" he said. "You knew, right?"

"Need to know, my man," Baptiste said with a cheery lilt. "No demonstrated need to know. You could do your job just fine without knowing that."

"So whenever you told us we were chopping off the head of the snake, this is what it was?" I said. "When we'd ID a leading element with an open gap behind it, and you'd tell us to calculate a next-day intercept point, you were setting us up to kill a bunch of teenage girls?"

Baptiste's smile tightened a notch. "What was it the colonel said yesterday? 'You played a key role in the elimination of enemy assets.' That's all you need to know, right? Hey, Buonacone — you got any of those fine cigars on you today? Think you could spare me one?"

Buonacone gave me a long look. I started to shrug, but that felt like a desecration, so I just stared back at him. Finally, he fished a cigar from a side pocket of his fatigue blouse. His hand shook.

Baptiste clamped the cigar in his teeth and grinned around it. "Got a light?" he said.

Buonacone's hand with the lighter shook so hard Baptiste had to move his head around to keep the cigar tip in the flame long enough to get it lit. He kept his eyes fixed warily on Buonacone's face, and a tiny flame danced in each eye.

After that, things pretty much went to hell between Buanacone and me. It didn't help that we made the stacked-up corpses of teenage girls a closed subject. The nights in the shop with nothing to do, and then the days when ten steps outside the barracks could soak you to the bone—all that enforced idleness didn't help either. Nor did thinking about the fifty thousand grunts out there in the rain with nothing much to occupy their minds, except the jungle rot eating up their feet or the ambush they might run into beyond the next tree line.

I made out all right for a while. I read a lot of Thomas Hardy. And I got a very short letter from the woman who was working as her newspaper's police reporter.

"This job is teaching me to rank men by how much I trust them," she wrote. "I still rank you at the top."

I wrote her back a still shorter letter: "Don't."

After that I quit writing to either woman for a while. I started caring more about Hardy than I did about them. I saw that Hardy's work, like ours, started to look like fate by the time one girl drowned in a weir, or when enough of them piled up at the jungle's edge.

Buonacone got on a weightlifting and boxing jag. One afternoon he came back from the Army gym reeking of Atomic Balm and lay on his bed with his eyes open and just his chest moving.

"You look like Mussolini lying in state," I told him.

I'd concluded he might as well have been, for conversational purposes, when finally he said:

"Benito never got the chance, pal."

His voice was as soft as the last voice you expect ever to hear if the associates of the man you've double-crossed invite you to take the midwatch air along the docks.

"Benito lay in state in the tummies of a lot-ta lit-tul alley dogs," he said.

I chose to let any existential rings from that go on expanding in silence. But I could tell Buonacone's gauge was way over in the red, so I was braced against the bulkhead when he blew.

"Stinking, filthy, wind-robbing bastards!"

He vaulted out of bed and gave me one glance. He looked as mean as a rhino with an enlarged prostate. Then he grabbed the box of Coronellas from his footlocker and charged out the door. In a little while, I heard a toilet flush. Then I heard a second flush, and a third.

In the mornings, Buonacone left for the gym before Thi-Thi woke me. He'd get back about three o'clock and lie on his bed without talking until it was time to go to chow and then to the shop. He didn't even have the baseball scores to look forward to anymore. Braddock College had finished its season with just six wins. Its 20-odd losses included one to a junior college team.

When Buonacone quit smoking, I started waiting for the other shoe to drop. While I waited I ran out of Hardy, and then I was down to zip also. I got my dream filter firmly enough in place to block out that stack of dead girls, but once a dream of a whole platoon of marching, singing, laughing girls crept in anyway. I tried instead to dream about the two women I'd written to, but I couldn't remember what they looked like. Sometimes I'd start to dream normally, but then the dream would shift to infrared. I might dream of Thi-Thi's smiling face, and then, like the waning of a moon and the ascendance of some dark star, her smile would fade and I would see instead a nebulous, faltering heart. Then the heart would recede, and I would see that it beat inside a gecko's body. Finally, a glittering metal object would hit the gecko's chin and the lizard would fly off into space. The only time I felt certifiably alive was during my daily tussle with Thi-Thi.

So when the other shoe hit for Buonacone, I was in no shape to help. He got smashed at the club and went to the steam-and-cream outside the gate. He'd sworn he'd never do that. When he got back, he sat on his bed with his face in his hands. I could see the talc on his neck and forearms. After a while I got sick of seeing him like that.

"Look, what's your grief?" I said. "She bite you? So hurry down to the clap shack while the marks are fresh. Maybe they'll give you a Purple Heart."

When he finally took his hands away from his face, I saw how bad it really was. His face looked like a bloated, ill-proportioned, roadside-art caricature of itself.

"Do you know what I think of you, Pete?" His voice had the dockside hush, but it sounded hoarse and broken now.

"I'm curious," I said. "But I doubt it's down there deep enough to countermine what I think of you."

"I think you're the kind of little yellow buttercup that would shoot himself in the foot the first time you saw a buddy come back down the hill in a rubber bag. I think they ought to rip your chevrons off, you lousy yellow shithook."

It dawned on me that he'd simply scooped up and flung a quick shovelful of the doubts that have assailed rear echelon troops ever since Hannibal's adjutant rounded up enough sad sacks to hold the elephants' reins while the grunts plunged on into the swamps at Cannae. I understood that. But my insight didn't make me feel more kindly disposed.

"Now shall we get on to what I think of you?" I said.

"No, because I'm not done yet."

I waited for him to pour the pesto sauce over what he thought of me.

"I almost said you were too yellow to climb into a ring with me. But I don't think that's right, pal. I think you're the kind that's too yellow to act like a straight-up coward. I think you'll go about a round and a half and then take your yellow dive."

Next morning Buonacone woke me by laying a hand gently on my shoulder.

"I'm sorry, Pete. I was blinko. You take my apology, buddy?"

Somewhere I loved Buonacone at that moment, but we were past the point where that could make a difference.

"You know, Arnaldo, for the first time in maybe ever, I regret that English lacks an intensive verb form."

The tenderness in his face congealed like sausage fat in a cold snap.

"Yeah? Why's that?"

"Because if it had one, I could tell you in it to go get as massaged as possible."

We went to the Army gym. In a small room off the gym floor was a boxing ring on a platform with canvas stretched across it and sandbags around the edges to hold the canvas tight. In a corner of the room was a rack of gloves, wrap tape and padded headgear. Buonacone wrapped his hands quickly and expertly and tossed me the roll of tape. I tossed it back.

"No thanks," I said.

He hadn't touched the headgear, but he glanced toward the rack and then raised his eyebrows at me quizzically. "Let's go," I said.

We climbed through the ropes. He unclasped the stainless steel watchband of his Rolex and looped it over a corner post of the ring. We pulled on the gloves.

"Three rounds, two minutes each?" he said.

From his softened tone, I understood we would spar in a gentlemanly semblance of boxing, and I could check the watch unmolested whenever I wished, and after three rounds of this swing-and-shuffle kabuki I could quit without disgrace. I remember thinking: time for a little daylight imagery.

"Hey, Arnaldo," I said. "That little girl who yanked or sucked you off, whichever it was—was she as cute as the ones we wasted?"

I stepped forward and punched him in the eye. I threw another punch and he swatted it aside. He had that pissed-off rhino look again.

After the first minute or so, it didn't hurt at all. It was like getting pelted with toy balloons while riding a roller coaster that snapped your head back and forth. You started to admire the colors of the balloons. You were still admiring them when they were coming up at you out of the canvas.

When Buonacone tried to lift me by the shoulders, I managed to backhand him with a glove and pull myself up by the ropes. His eyes narrowed and his breath quickened. It was about then that I figured out where this fight needed to take us.

He feinted left and followed with a roundhouse hook, and blood from my nose spattered the canvas. I pointed down at it.

"One hundred probable troops!" I said, laughing. Arnaldo gave me a puzzled frown. Then he started laughing, too. He lowered his guard, leaving me a clear shot, and I gave him a hard left to the face. He sloshed the blood around in his mouth, then spat out a glob of it that landed halfway across the ring. He pointed at it, spattering more blood as he laughed.

"Eight probable buffalo, yoked two-by-two!"

We kept that up, punching each other and spitting blood and giving it the kinds of names we'd written down in block letters all dry season long, based on nothing but mental coin-flips. Whenever one of us spat blood, we both laughed in big, jackass brays, since the blood was nobody's but our own. Finally, when I saw Arnaldo's nostrils were clogged with it, I waved at him to cease fire. I pulled off my gloves, pincered his nose with two fingers and stripped clots from his nostrils into my other palm. Then I flung them onto the canvas between us.

"Fifty sixteen-year-old girls!" I said, pointing at the little mound they'd made. "Their sandbox shovels are down in there somewhere, too." We weren't laughing any more.

"Probable?" Arnaldo said.

"Confirmed."

Buonacone took his Rolex off the post and climbed through the ropes, and I tossed him my gloves.

"Don't we need to do something about the blood?" I said.

"Neg-a-tive," he said. "One thing you can say for the Army, they got beaucoup canvas. We bloody it up, they peel it off and replace."

I climbed out of the ring and stumbled across the gym's tile floor, holding out the bottom of my T-shirt to catch the blood dripping from my nose. I kept holding out the shirt all the way to the barracks, watching the dark, wet blooms expand in the blazing sunlight, then vanish into the olive cloth.

When Buonacone got back, he was carrying a wooden cigar box about twice the size of his usual box of Coronellas. This one looked big and solid enough to safely transport tarantulas.

Buonacone had a swollen, purple eyelid and splits in both lips. He'd found cotton to stuff up his nose. He sat on his bed without looking at me and levered loose the nail in the box lid with the flat, slotted end of his gun-cleaning rod. From the box he took a slightly crooked and very black cigar. He lit it, and the atmosphere quickly approached a windless day in Newark. The fumes' specific gravity must have been pretty high. The maids on the lower deck started coughing.

At six o'clock, we took our faces to the shop. At midnight, Sergeant Baptiste came to tell us we could go. He clomped up the steps and issued his customary greeting, "good eeeve-ning," before he got a good look at us. Then he just stood there, staring back and forth between our faces. He looked like he was about to say something when Buonacone whipped out one of his crooked black stogies, stuck it in Baptiste's mouth and lit it with a steady hand.

Baptiste took two puffs, then bent double in a fit of wheezing coughs. Each wheeze lasted so long you wondered how he found more breath to expire. Buonacone leaned over far enough to get face-to-face with him. They would have been eye-to-eye, too, except that Buonacone's near eye was swollen shut and Baptiste, still wheezing, was staring bug-eyed at the floor.

"Oh, oh, oh, Sarge, I forgot to say 'may I,' didn't I?" Buonacone said. "My fuckup, okay? I'll do better next time. Because—see, now you've demonstrated a need to know!"

Halfway through the rainy season, they started routing us daylight aerial photography of the DMZ for secondary interpretation. It was a snap. If you saw tanks or trucks or bunkers or people, you just wrote down what you saw. No more staring yourself stoned at a string of blobs and shuffling through intel reports and getting interrogation section on the horn to ask if they had anything new on troop movements or Lao tribesmen in that sector, and finally making a guess that you couldn't even call educated—and suspecting all the while that there wasn't really anything at all down there that you could fit a name to, but rather some nameless nocturnal essence. We didn't see any more piled-up corpses, or any sign of an all-girl road crew.

"Good chance the Girl Scouts in Hanoi quit offering that merit badge," Baptiste said. "None of those little mama-sans was staying alive long enough to sew one on her sash anyway."

Thi-Thi still set off her primitive digital alarm each day, until the morning our dalliance stopped.

"That's loosening up the old members, Thi-Thi!" Buonacone bellowed when he heard the twin report from my yanked toes. "That's givin' him a foretaste of ecs-tasy untold!"

I told him to go catechize the big rat that frequented the head. He took his toilet kit from his footlocker and said it was no use trying to pin patrimony on him, since he was logging his morning visits to the head and getting the log notarized.

Balanced catlike on the balls of his sandaled feet, Buonacone paused in the cubicle doorway, and Arnaldo and Thi-Thi smiled at each other. Both smiles were subdued, but beautiful. It was like two Florentine Madonnas facing each other from adjoining walls of a museum, if one of them had an exhumed cigar shoved in its jaw. Then he was gone down the hall, proclaiming he would serve as godfather only if we agreed to the name Antipasto.

When I leapt at Thi-Thi, she hopped on the unsnared foot once before she froze, her hand to her breast, her shoulders hunched as though she were about to cough. But she didn't cough. When I heard that she wasn't panting either, I let go of her ankle and held her shoulders. She was still smiling but her eyes looked dry and lost. Then she breathed again, in harsh gasps, and I heard her teeth grind.

I made her sit on the bed. She rubbed the heel of a hand across her breastbone until the gasping subsided.

"Don't you have some medicine?" I mimed the unscrewing of a bottle cap and the shaking out and swallowing of a pill. From her breast I felt a secret, halting glow, as I would feel the dark glow when I reeled up a nocturnal convoy.

She gave an abashed nod and tried to stand, but I held her arms. "No. I'll get it."

I tried to make her lie down, but she said something quick and imploring and swung her feet back to the floor. I went downstairs to the end of the barracks where the maids left their things, and I hunted in her tattered plastic bag. There were shoe polish tins and laundry powder. A jar of rice flecked with meat and peppers. A brush and metal comb for when she would wash her hair in the evening, swinging her wet hair in a gleaming arc back from one of the big metal garbage cans the maids used for laundry and—laughing and gabbling and splashing—for washing their hair between the barracks where the dust from the street wouldn't reach them. I found two white tablets wrapped in a torn bit of newspaper, and I got a paper cone of water from the cooler.

From the stairwell I heard Thi-Thi's harsh but steady breathing and Buonacone speaking softly to her. I stopped short when I turned the corner of our cubicle, and a little water slopped from the paper cone. Buonacone had scooped her up with one arm beneath her knees and the other below her shoulders. He stood with his back to the doorway, feet apart in a good batter's stance, rocking her gently back and forth. Her little bare feet peeked out when he swung her one way, and a bit of ponytail flipped past his shoulder when he swung her the other.

I was about to bawl at him, *Don't do that! Worst thing possible!* But then I thought: big picture, maybe not.

"You're gonna be okay, Thi-Thi," he said, in a tone as close to tender as his gravelly wop voice would stretch. "I gotcha. I gotcha now. We're not gonna let you die."

Cadence Count

Of the months after the bus to Fort Bragg disgorged him and the other recruits it had picked up at a half-dozen county draft board buildings en route, Peter Dandridge would later remember little about the strictly military parts, except disappointment. He remembered how promptly and completely the Army fulfilled his father's warning to expect an environment "profane beyond belief." He remembered with a mix of resignation and gratitude that he'd been able to make good on the promise he'd made to his mother that he would, if possible, steer clear of a combat assignment. Far above the rest of it, he remembered Leon and Wilshire—remembered them in the way he might from time to time have pondered a strange coin bearing the likeness of Janus, the two-faced Roman god of all beginnings, trying to unlock its mystery.

The full-pack road marches, crawling beneath live machine-gun fire and midnight guard duty shifts hadn't risen to the level of hardship set by the two-a-day football practices, often sandwiched around hours of hay-baling, that he'd endured in high school. About halfway through his nine weeks of basic training, word came down that college graduates could interview for teaching jobs at the Vietnamese air academy in Quan Rang. Sergeant Wilshire, the older and more droopy-eyed of their two drill sergeants, read out the notice at morning muster. Peter interviewed with a fifty-ish civilian from the Defense Language Institute who told him the teaching was all "direct-method," meaning teachers used only English in the classroom.

"Once you finish basic, you'll probably be in a holding pattern for more than a month before the next training class starts up," the man said. "That could work to your advantage."

"An advantage in that much dead time?" Peter said.

The man had a salt-and-pepper mustache cut flush with the corners of his mouth and the raffish smile of a man with something up his sleeve.

"You're a draftee, right?" he said. "If you come home from the Nam with less than six months left on your enlistment and your service record is clean, normally the Army will give you an early discharge. They don't need your job specialty anywhere in the States, and it's not worth the Army's nickel to retrain a troop with so little time left to serve. Once you finish your six weeks of instructor training, you can expect a couple of weeks' home leave before you ship out. The normal tour in Vietnam for all the branches except the jarheads is one year, but you'll have some discretion. You can probably get your rotation date set several weeks beyond the one-year mark. Over there, the Army is getting the only good use they're ever going to get from you, right? Why wouldn't they let you stay on for a little extra time? Right? So do the math."

Peter did the math. "When do I have to let you know?" he said.

The man swirled his coffee. The trickster smile stayed fixed and his eyes narrowed a little.

"You're just what we're looking for," he said. "Strong college record, certified to teach. For us, the crème de la crème would be a guy with an ESL degree, but damned few of those are going to turn up in Army basic training. So I'd say that if you sign this form right now, you're a lock." He edged the paper toward Peter's side of the desk and tapped a forefinger against the signature line.

"All right," Peter said. "Let's say I sign this form, but later another opportunity opens up. Could I still switch?"

Beneath the salt-and-pepper mustache, Peter saw the glint of teeth, and the man's tone of voice shifted from wily to annoyed.

"My friend, this is the U.S. Army," he said. "At any given time, you've got about a quarter million little marbles bouncing around in a thousand roulette wheels, and who's to say which slot any of those little marbles will tumble down into? All I can tell you is that, of the men I've signed up as language trainers for Vietnam, so far as I know, every mother's son of them has ended up in that assignment."

Cerberus, Peter thought. Guarding the entrance to the underworld. Letting faint, shivering shades like me pass through, but letting none of them out again. He signed the form volunteering to teach English in Vietnam.

Over against his sense of resignation that any chance he would have to display a militarily stalwart heart had now been snuffed out, Peter had Leon. In fact, as Peter came to understand, over against whatever disappointment or fear or sense of irretrievable loss anyone in the training platoon suffered, that was what they all had: Leon. On Peter's first morning in the barracks, when the recruits snapped to attention in their underwear as their two drill sergeants stormed down the lane between the bunks, shouting that they were all lower than whale shit, which was at the bottom of the sea, Peter became uneasily aware that he had never stood so close to anyone as Black as the man to his left. When the sergeants had stormed downstairs to harangue the recruits on the first floor and Peter was free to turn and look at him, Leon Meriwether was already laughing, head thrown back and clapping his hands in a loose-jointed rhythm.

"Oh, man!" Leon said, still laughing. "*Whale* shit! We've just stepped through the looking glass, y'all. We'd better find a way to enjoy ourselves on this side. Let's get to work on that, now."

The second thing Peter noticed about Leon, after the gleaming, obsidian Blackness of his skin, was the gap between his upper two front teeth. Later that first day, while they were policing the ground around the barracks for cigarette butts and other trash, another recruit from their floor asked Leon to demonstrate how far he could spit through that gap.

None of them had yet been issued uniforms or had their hair cut. The one who had asked Leon to spit was a little towhead wearing a T-shirt emblazoned with a burning cross on the front and "Impeach Earl Warren" on the back.

"Never did spit much, between the teeth or any other way," Leon said. "I can show you what else those teeth are good for, though."

"Yeah?" the little towhead said guardedly. He dragged one foot behind the other, as though he might launch himself at Leon. "You're not about to go and get smart with me now, are you, Black boy?"

"Oh, Jesus," Peter muttered, summoning the muscle memory he would need to throw a forearm block into the little redneck. But Leon reacted swiftly, gently grasping the smaller man's wrist and laughing with his head thrown back.

"No, no, man! This is something you may even like! Now listen." In a sweet, clear tenor, Leon sang a couple of bars from the ballad Otis Redding composed while sitting on a rented houseboat in San Francisco Bay. Then Leon performed the song's whistle lines through that gap in his teeth. Unlike the shrill whistle on Redding's recording, however, Leon's was so deep and resonant that it resembled a foghorn.

A perfect touch, Peter thought, for that song. The other men, slowly prowling the bare ground and occasionally bending to pluck something from it, paused and stood upright to listen, like a gaggle of suddenly alerted shore birds. Finally, Leon performed a little of the song's bass line with a combination of humming and glottal stops. When he was done, he smiled at the little towhead and said, "See? God don't give you grillwork like mine for no good reason. You've just got to figure out what it's for."

Leon bunked next to Peter. While the two of them were sitting on their footlockers polishing their just-issued combat boots, Leon told Peter he'd been able to complete a master's degree in music education at Chapel Hill before his draft deferment ran out. And Peter learned that, like himself, Leon didn't really want to teach. He had a wife and a baby boy, and they were back in Wilmington now, living with his parents. Leon's father had come to Wilmington from Jamaica in the 1940s. Leon said that back then, after a country club in Wilmington lost its chef to the draft, one of the club officers had suggested they make Caribbean cuisine a selling point to recruit new members. Incidentally, the club officer said, he knew of a terrific chef at a restaurant in Kingston, Jamaica, who could make that happen.

Peter asked Leon if he would angle for assignment to an Army band, and Leon laughed and shook his head. "No way," he said. "I don't play any band instrument, just piano and harpsichord. The only music to march by I could ever make is the kind you heard me do while we were picking up butts to keep our country safe. I can do something else with that kind of music, and when the time seems right, maybe I'll wheel that out. Something I taught myself to do, just because I had the physical equipment to do it. And it might fit in real well on this side of the looking glass. But Army musician? No, I want to be a top-tier Army cook. I'm a pretty good chef already. I filled in a lot as sous chef when my dad's regular guy was on vacation, and for the past couple of years I've cooked part-time at the Carolina Inn. If I can get posted to some high-end officers' club, maybe I can get up close enough to my dad's skill level that he'll bring me on as full-time sous when I muster out. Blood relative or no, if I can't sauté over here and flambé over there, and get a half dozen other orders started in between and have it all come our perfect, there's no way he'd give me that job. So no Army band for me. If some Army band leader did get hold of me, know what he'd do? He'd listen to my voice a little bit and then he'd take a long, hard look at my complexion. And then this beatific glow would come into his face and he'd say, 'I know what! We'll have you sing Nat King Cole numbers at officers' club dances and ROTC balls on college campuses for the next two years!' And I'd be miserable doing that. I'm partial to baroque music—Bach, Telemann. There's no market for that music in the U.S. Army."

But it took less than a week for Leon to secure his place as the rhythmically beating heart of the training platoon. The two drill sergeants briefly begrudged him that status until it seemed that they, too, were seduced by the witchery of his music.

One day when the sun blazed down with such intensity that all trainees were ordered to sit on their footlockers during what otherwise would have been an hour of drill, Leon demonstrated the art of hambone. Seated on his locker, he slapped his thighs, chest, shoulders and elbows in a rhythm he set with one tapping heel. Then he gradually sped up the rhythm until his hands were a blur and the men sitting on their lockers hooted with glee, and those from the barracks' first floor crowded through the doorway to watch. Leon told Peter he learned hambone from his father, only his father had called it juba and said he'd learned it from cane-cutters in the Jamaican village where he'd grown up.

They marched to cadence calls, many of them obscene, that LaFarge, the younger and less hangdog-looking of the two drill sergeants, sang out. Peter found the chants engaging until he realized they were recycling endlessly through the sergeant's small repertoire. Peter found the chants that featured a back-home rapscallion named Jody groaningly dull. He liked the brief, to-the-point, chants best.

"I don't know, but I've been told
I don't know, but I've been told
Eskimo pussy is mighty cold
Eskimo pussy is mighty cold

Leon laughed and chanted as heartily as the rest of them at lyrics like those. Peter found this puzzling until he figured out that, while Leon had exacting tastes, neither snobbery nor prudery had much to do with them.

Leon incorporated some of those cadence calls into his hambone routines, which he varied to create constant surprise. Those routines quickly became a regular nightly feature for the men in the barracks. When the two drill sergeants had wearied of demanding that toilets be scrubbed until they were clean enough to make a sandwich on the seats, they would delay lights-out long enough for Leon to perform his latest creation. For a couple of nights, the sergeants wore disapproving frowns as they lingered in the doorway by the stairwell. Then one night, as Leon was winding up his routine and all that could be seen of his flying hands was a blur between his shoulders and knees, Peter saw the two sergeants glance at each other. Wilshire's lips moved, forming the clearly discernible words, "What the hell?" Then, as Leon leaned back, exhausted, against the metal railing at the foot of his bunk, the other sergeant, LaFarge, laughed and clapped along with the trainees. But Wilshire, Peter remembered, simply kept looking at Leon, and he squinted a little, as if he were pondering possibilities. Peter remembered, too, that it was then he noticed that, while LaFarge wore three chevrons on his collar, Wilshire was just one step higher in rank, with a single rocker below his chevrons. Peter wondered why Wilshire, who appeared much the elder of the two, should be stuck in the rank of staff sergeant.

One night about two weeks in, after Leon had done the hambone to the usual cheers and laughter and LaFarge had doused the lights and all the recruits were in their bunks, Peter asked Leon if he felt he was being boxed into putting on a nightly minstrel show.

"I don't look at it that way, man," Leon said. "Remember our first morning here, when they screamed and called us whale shit, and I said we'd better look for ways to enjoy life on this side of the looking glass? The way I look at it, I'm just doing the best I can to make that happen."

Leon gave no hint he had more revelations to unveil until their drill sergeants herded them all into Womack Army Hospital to get a barrage of inoculations fired with air guns into both arms. As they shuffled through the corridors, Peter recognized the intersection where, on the day months earlier when an orthopedist had ruled him draft-eligible despite the knee injury he'd suffered in football, he had seen approaching what seemed to him the human equivalent of driven sheep. Now, he realized, to any other first-time visitor, his own sweating, exhausted-looking face set off by his sunburned neck and close-cropped hair must seem as devoid of any higher human quality as all those frightened young faces had seemed to him then.

Then, from well back in the crowd of recruits behind him, Peter heard it. He immediately knew who it was and what had to be done to produce it, though he couldn't understand how anyone could actually do that. It was a Bach two-part invention—he could tell that much. Leon was creating the bass line with deep-throated humming and glottal stops, the same way he had done with the Otis Redding song outside the barracks that day. Through that gap in his teeth he was whistling the notes Bach had set down in the treble clef, just as he had done with Redding's whistle lines. But Leon was performing both parts simultaneously, in perfect counterpoint.

A nurse hurrying along one of the hallways stopped and turned full-circle in bewilderment, looking for the source of what must seem to her the unlikeliest sounds imaginable in those corridors. Peter was sure all the members of his platoon did know where those sounds were coming from. And he didn't even have to look at them to know that the music glowed in their faces. Now, they would realize, they were not just sheep-faced integers borne along on a vast processing line toward a distant market, where some of their lives would be exchanged for what someone somewhere must count as currency worth the cost. Instead, in that counterpoint between Leon's deep humming and the clarinet-like resonance of his whistling, each of them could find the exact value of his own soul, calculable in no currency other than the music itself.

After the air guns had peppered their arms from shoulder to bicep and their drill sergeants had marched them to the mess hall, the little towhead managed to edge his way into the chow line just behind Peter.

"Hey, you're pretty tight, aren't you, with that Meriwether, that Black dude who does the clown act in the barracks?" the towhead said.

"What?" Peter said. Turning, he saw that the name sewn over a breast pocket of the towhead's fatigue blouse was Simpson. "Oh. Well, yeah. His bunk's right next to mine, so we get to talk a lot."

"Well." Simpson's voice dropped a little. "Does he ever try to put a move on you?"

"A move on me?" Peter said, suspecting he knew what was meant and wanting to be wrong. "Sorry, I don't know what you're talking about."

"Well, that was him making that weirdo music in the hospital just before we got our shots, right? I already figured he was probably queer-boots, but after what he done back there in the hospital, I'm sure of it."

Peter chuckled, trying hard to channel his fury into the semblance of amusement.

"Well, you'll have to ask him, and I suggest you do that. What makes you think that, just because he makes music like that, he has to be—what was that word you used?"

"Queer-boots. Because Black dudes never make music like that. They all sing soul music, except some of the older ones from back in the country, and they might sing gospel. That song he was doing outside the barracks that day? That was maybe all right. But whatever that was he was doing back there in the hospital? That was definitely queer-boots for a Black dude to do that. In fact, I think any male person, even a white one, that could make sounds like that come out of his mouth would have to be a queer."

Later that afternoon, they shouldered their rubber ducks—mock M16 rifles their sergeants made them drill with, and occasionally sleep with—and they boarded buses to the firing range. Waiting in line to board their bus, Peter warned Leon that the little towhead, Simpson, was likely to make trouble for him. When Peter told him what sort of trouble, Leon put one hand on the back of his neck, leaned his head backward and shut his eyes. For a few seconds he appeared lost in thought.

"So if I'd just done 'Papa's Got a Brand New Bag' back there in the hospital, he'd have been fine with that?" Leon said.

"I don't think it's that," Peter said. "I think it's that you're Black and you don't behave exactly like any of the Black people he's encountered back in whatever pinhead- and pellagra-ridden swamp he crawled up out of."

"I see," Leon said. He gave several sharp tugs to the back of his neck, until he got what he seemed to regard as a satisfactory pop from his neck bone. "Well, sometimes we just have to put our faith in the overarching goodness of creation, or in whatever part of it we find ourselves stuck in at the moment."

Sergeant Wilshire mounted the bottom step of the bus and turned to face the line of recruits. Wilshire had a missing earlobe, and Peter had noticed he always tilted that side of his face forward when berating recruits, as if to add a soupçon of intimidation that his hangdog expression alone failed to sufficiently convey. In the mock-furious voice that seemed to be the chief and, in some cases, only qualification of Army drill instructors, Wilshire shouted that if anyone planned to board his bus without making sure his weapon's safety was on, he might as well bend over right then and kiss his ass goodbye.

"A part of creation—," Leon said, quickly checking the safety switch on his rubber duck and bringing the dummy weapon to the required present-arms position, "—which happens at this moment to be, praise Jesus, the United States Army."

From their prior visits to the firing range and from bewildered-sounding testimony from other recruits, Peter knew to expect a Zen-like change in Sergeant Wilshire once they were issued clips with live rounds and loaded them and lay prone, waiting for the range sergeant's command to open fire. You always knew when it was Wilshire who had stepped beside you on the firing line because of the absurd length of his bootlaces, which were triple-wrapped around the tops of his combat boots. Also because Wilshire would speak to you only if he saw some hint of either fear or overexcitement as you were sighting downrange. Then he would lean behind you and speak in a voice so low and soft that you might imagine it was coming from somewhere inside your own skull instead of from the graying little man in the Smokey Bear hat who had a missing earlobe and pouches that hung like empty saddlebags beneath his eyes. He would tell you in that inside-your-head voice to relax because your weapon knew the bond between itself and you was eternal, sacred and inviolable, and the spirit of your weapon had in fact snuggled next to you as a cradle-mate, and the man your weapon would someday enable you to kill in combat had already forgiven you, and so had his parents and wife and children, although they didn't know it yet, but your weapon did know it and had already placed its seal on a guarantee of absolution that would be handed over to any interested authorities, earthly or divine. One recruit told Peter that Wilshire's soothing voice had made him forget he was using a firing-range weapon and that any long-term relationship with it was impossible.

At the firing range, Wilshire told them to leave their dummy weapons on the bus. For two hours they practiced with live-fire weapons they propped on sandbags. Peter noticed that Sergeant Wilshire spent a lot of time hovering over someone several positions down the firing line. Only later, when the range master gave the order to clear weapons, remove magazines and engage safeties, did Peter see that the object of Wilshire's attention had been Simpson.

Wilshire had them retrieve their dummy weapons from the bus, line up outside and then reboard the bus with the rubber ducks' safeties flipped on. As Peter and Leon stepped past him at the bus's door, Wilshire told them to report to what he called his office as soon as they got back to the barracks. The cubicle contained a desk, chair and tackboard, leaving barely enough room for the three of them to edge into it. Wilshire shut the door and gave them a perfunctory snarling order not to look at him. Peter and Leon came to attention and stared above the sergeant's head. Wilshire spoke to them in a near-whisper, though the snarl stayed in it.

"Out on the firing range today, one of your fellow pieces of shit, a remarkably small piece of it, told me that one of you has—oh, how shall I put this?—has a propensity widely viewed as incompatible with honorable military service," he said. "I reminded him that butt-fucking and proper operation of an M16 are mutually exclusive categories, and confusing the two on a firing range could prove hazardous to one's own or a fellow soldier's health. But the little turd would have blown the balls off half the platoon before he'd let go of his point. He cited what he claimed was evidence. I told him my beloved Jolly Green Giant, the U.S. Army, made a dire mistake ever allowing him to raise his right hand for any purpose other than to pick his nose. But he still wouldn't let it go, and he said that the other one of you could confirm what he was saying."

"Drill sergeant, Simpson has already aired his accusation with me," Peter said. "And I assure you, drill sergeant, there's not a single part of what he's telling you—"

Wilshire's sunburned, basset-eyed face bulged up into Peter's line of sight. "Did I ask you to respond, dick-face?" he said in a menacing whisper. "If the two of you will pool your individual quarter-rations of brainpower, you will notice I did not ask you for either confirmation or denial. Do you notice, too, that I did not even mention which of you was which in this scenario spelled out to me by your ever-loyal comrade in arms? I'm simply conveying information to you in a spirit as close to loving-kindness as I can muster toward two individuals who remind me so strongly of cancer: slow, and completely unwanted."

Wilshire took a sideways step toward Leon and shoved his face upward as close as Leon's as possible, given their difference in height.

"However, I do want a direct answer to one question, and I want it from you," Wilshire said. "Can you march backward, sing and whistle all at the same time?"

Peter thought Wilshire must be trying to blindside Leon and thereby extract from him some sort of confession. Leon must have thought the same thing, because, after a moment's hesitation, he said, slowly and calmly, "No, drill sergeant. I think I understand what you're asking, and yes, I can sing and whistle at the same time. But no, I don't walk backward. Never had any inclination that way, drill sergeant."

Wilshire reentered Peter's line of sight. The sergeant was shaking his head in mock wonderment.

"You make me believe in reincarnation," he said. "Nobody could get that stupid in just one lifetime. Listen again to my question: Can you sing and whistle, the way you were doing earlier today in the hospital, and can you march backward while you're doing that?"

"Sure, I can do that, drill sergeant," Leon said warily. "I can't imagine why I would need to do it, but—"

"Then don't try," Wilshire said, reverting to the tone and volume he would use out on the barracks floor. "I wouldn't want you to strain your feeble mental capacity trying to imagine that or anything else. I think we're done here. Now get out of my house."

Like A Wary Blessing

A couple of days later at pugil-stick practice, Sergeant Wilshire stood with his arms folded beside the low wooden platform, watching the recruits, clad in football helmets, hockey gloves and padding for their chests and hips, batter each other with sticks heavily padded at either end. On the platform, Sergeant LaFarge demonstrated for each new pair of combatants the footwork prescribed for an infantryman preparing to thrust his bayonet into an enemy's chest or gut. The footwork reminded Peter of the strutting approach of a barnyard rooster. When Simpson mounted the platform, Wilshire abruptly stepped forward and grabbed the arm of the man in line behind Simpson and told him to wait. Then Wilshire pointed down the line at Leon and waved him forward. He said something in Leon's ear and nudged him on toward the platform.

Rather than mimic LaFarge's footwork, which involved dragging the back foot along the floor like a boxer, Simpson started bounding about the floor like a cricket. Ducking and weaving, he feinted with the padded ends of his stick as if they were boxing gloves. Leon flicked these blows aside, standing still and barely moving his own stick and turning his eyes toward Wilshire whenever Simpson retreated out of range. Finally, Peter saw Wilshire tilt his head at Leon, who moved swiftly forward in the drag-footed gait LaFarge had modeled. Holding his stick at a slight upward angle, he drove the red-painted padding that indicated the bayonet end of his stick squarely into Simpson's chest. Simpson, caught at the apogee of a cricket-leap, was lifted still higher off the floor and landed on his back on the ground outside the platform.

Simpson instantly sprang to his feet, and Peter saw his face redden as the line of men convulsed with laughter. LaFarge again waved Simpson forward onto the platform. All the men were asked to do two or three rounds, or as many as it took for LaFarge to express satisfaction with their performance or give up on them as hopeless. Simpson's second and third rounds were near-duplicates of his first, including Wilshire's silent cue to Leon and Leon's swift eviction of Simpson from the platform, though both times Simpson did manage to land on his feet instead of his back. Round four looked to Peter like more of the same, though the spring was ebbing from Simpson's cricket-leaps and his bobbing and weaving bespoke resignation more than swagger. This time, though, it looked to Peter like Wilshire gave Leon a different, more emphatic nod. Leon responded by advancing on Simpson slowly and with both ends of the pugil stick held side-to-side, in sparring position. When they engaged—Simpson flailing wildly and Leon deftly deflecting the blows—Leon retreated carefully until, at the floor's edge, he appeared to misjudge the angle of Simpson's next swipe. It caught Leon on the side of the helmet and seemed to knock him far enough off balance that he had to step down from the edge. The watching members of the platoon cheered Simpson as loudly as earlier they had laughed at him, and instantly his square-shouldered swagger returned. LaFarge blew his whistle to summon the next pair of combatants. As Leon and Simpson handed over the pugil sticks, Leon stuck out his hand, and Simpson seized it and shook it.

Without looking at Peter, Wilshire stepped close to where Peter stood in the line of men waiting their turn at the pugil sticks.

"That should take care of that," Wilshire said, just loud enough for Peter to hear, though still without looking at him. "Simple measures for simple minds."

~ * ~

They were in the sixth of their nine weeks of basic training now. Wilshire had told them it would be near the end—maybe at the very end—before they would learn their duty assignments.

"For many, if not most of you, it's going to be some charming variation on the grand old theme of combat arms," he told them. "That's just the get-down groove the Green Giant has got down into, and you might as well prepare yourselves to get down there with him, to the merry old rhythm of a-rat-a-tat-tat."

One evening in that sixth week, Sergeant Wilshire stuck his head in the doorway at the end of Peter's floor and ordered Peter and Leon to get their boots on and report to him outside immediately, if not sooner. Earlier that day, Wilshire had turned the platoon over to LaFarge, saying he had an urgent scrounging mission that might benefit them all.

Peter paused a moment when he stepped out onto the second-floor landing. When the teacher in his high school art class had asked the students to think of their favorite subject for a still life and then make a sketch of it, Peter had chosen a forest landscape of longleaf pines and yellow wiregrass. Nothing in what he knew of the natural world seemed to him as geometrically pure yet suggestive of hidden mystery as those forests of widely spaced, sentinel-like pines that his family drove through on their summertime trips to Holden's Beach. It was the longleaf pines, he knew, that had made him feel strangely at home throughout what were intended as the disorienting pressures of basic training. As he stepped onto the landing, he first fixed his eyes, as he always did, on the tops of the distant pines. They were brilliantly lit by a blaze from the setting sun. Then he heard Sergeant Wilshire's electrically amplified voice: "They say every child gets fertilized by the fastest sperm. You two fuckheads might be the only exceptions on the biological record."

Peter and Leon clattered down the steps and came to attention facing Wilshire, who was breathing hard in feigned fury and holding what Peter took to be a compact, battery-powered megaphone. Wilshire thrust his face up toward Leon's with that sideways tilt of the head that directed verbal abuse into one of the target's ears and thereby, drill sergeants seemed to feel, heightened its persuasive power.

"Why I ask someone of your intellectual caliber to even attempt this is beyond me," Wilshire said. "If you fell into a barrel of size D titties, you'd probably come out sucking your thumb. Nonetheless, the potential gain here warrants the wager. All you have to do is march backward, hold this instrument up to your mouth—pretend it's an interestingly shaped, battery-powered dick if that helps you—and do your mongoloid throat singing and whistling through that wind tunnel where normal human beings have their front teeth. You got that?"

Wilshire told Peter that, when Leon started marching backward, he should march forward at a constant twenty-yard interval behind Leon and make mental note of whether he could hear Leon clearly and whether Leon was setting a good marching cadence. Then he told

Peter to stay put while he led Leon about twenty yards up the street between the rows of recruit barracks. He handed Leon the battery-powered megaphone and showed him how to switch it on.

"I will now quote your mama's command to your papa during foreplay, right after she'd drunk enough Draino to extinguish brain activity in any resulting offspring, which sadly turned out to be you," Wilshire said. "Proceed."

Leon didn't attempt any music at first. He and Wilshire began marching backward in tandem, Leon at first stepping cautiously and Wilshire swatting Leon's elbow several times and pointing down at his own legs as models of the proper length and height of each step. In the fading light, Wilshire's triple-wrapped laces resembled solid bands around his boot tops. Peter just stood and watched until a furious summoning motion from Wilshire reminded him he was supposed to keep pace, and he double-timed to restore the proper interval.

After about a minute Leon seemed to feel enough at ease with backward marching to give the music a try. At first his whistling and humming and the plucked notes from his vocal cords were all but drowned out by the surf-like roar of his breath against the mouthpiece, but after another round of furious gesturing by Wilshire, Leon moved the megaphone further from his lips. Then Peter could recognize the music. It was Bach's first two-part invention, sounding a little tinny and overloud through the megaphone. Peter remembered he'd heard it being played on the piano in the music room in his second year of high school when he passed it during lunch period on the way to get a book from his locker. He had opened the music room door and learned then that Delores Fowler, a girl for whom his dewy fondness had never evolved into a full-blown crush, always went there to practice on the piano during lunch period. The money that lunch would have cost her she spent instead on sheet music. It was from that moment that Peter realized the hunger for art, beauty, can cut more sharply than hunger for food, and that those who suffer that heart-hunger will find a way to feed it, even if they have to do it secretly behind a music room door in an hour when no one is likely to pass by. And then, remembering how Delores had found a way to feed that hunger, Peter's body jerked like Galvani's frog's leg as the thought struck him: Wilshire, too? Good God, can somebody like Wilshire feel that, too?

By the time Leon and Sergeant Wilshire reached the end of the block of barracks, Leon had finished the first Bach invention. Both of them seemed satisfied with the pacing of his backward march-step. Peter heard an occasional bewildered "What the fuck?" from barracks as they passed, but for the most part, the clusters of recruits that appeared on barracks' landings watched and listened in silence. Wilshire guided Leon onto an intersecting street, both of them still marching backward but Leon no longer making any music.

"What happened to my cadence, dickhead?" Wilshire said. "You last no longer than that with your wife and she won't even notice she's been fucked."

Leon did another Bach two-part invention, and he segued into something also two-part but slower and simpler, before they started down the third side of the block of barracks they were apparently circumnavigating. Wilshire was growling "hut, hut, hut" and nodding in seeming approval of Leon's success in matching that cadence. From somewhere ahead, Peter heard the throttled-down engine of the mosquito spray truck. On the fourth leg, Peter's throat started to constrict from breathing the insecticide. When he turned a final corner and headed up the street toward their own barracks, he was coughing and he could barely see Leon and Wilshire up ahead, marching backward through the cloud of mosquito spray like pipers through the mists of Brigadoon. Leon was still at it. Except for that single early lapse, he had hummed and whistled enough continuous, high-baroque cadence to cover what Peter estimated would amount to a 20-minute march, though now Leon was winding down with a jingle from a television game show.

Sergeant Wilshire called a halt at the foot of the barracks steps, and Leon bent over abruptly and started to cough. When Peter caught up with them, Leon was still coughing and his fatigue blouse looked saturated with sweat from the waist up.

"Didn't Rachel Carson write a book about birds that cough their guts out when you expose them to a little bug spray?" Wilshire said.

"Maybe that's the source of my problem with the two of you. All this time I've been using human psychology on you, when what I needed was ornithology."

Peter reported that the music Leon made over the megaphone could be clearly heard in the rear rank of a marching platoon. Wilshire nodded and took the megaphone from Leon and switched it off. He waited until Leon was able to straighten up, and then he glared at Leon and Peter until they quit coughing and stood at attention.

"I strongly suspect that little piece of shit up there in the barracks is onto something about you," Wilshire told Leon in a soft snarl. "I almost said piece of dog shit, but that would be defamatory of man's best friend. Personally, I don't care if you're AC/DC or what you are. More importantly, the Jolly Green Giant doesn't care either. He's decided what he wants in his army is somebody who can perform Bach and Telemann with nothing but his mouth while he's marching backward. And, God help us, that turns out to be you. Dismissed."

Leon was peppered with questions as soon as they walked in the door. He had the same answer for them all.

"You saw it, you heard it," he said. "You know as much as I do about why he wants it."

Leon climbed the rungs to his upper bunk and fell face-forward on the mattress without even taking off his boots. Peter sat on his footlocker, looking up at Leon.

"He knew every one of them," Leon said, his eyes stark open, sweat streaming from his face onto his pillow.

"Every one of what?" Peter said.

"All the pieces of music he wanted. He wanted Bach's First and the Eighth and Fourteenth Two-Part Inventions and the Telemann Flute Sonata in G. When I couldn't recall how the Telemann starts, he whistled the first bar of the flute line until it clicked with me."

"He must have just studied up on that music somehow," Peter said.

"No, Pete. I think there's something occult going on here. The last six years up in Chapel Hill, I was this eccentric Black guy who just wanted to study old music and play the harpsichord and learn to be a top-tier chef. I figured I was what the Brits call a complete one-off. No way could I ever suspect that just down the road in Fayetteville I had this evil-twin white Army sergeant who'd learned the same music better than I ever learned it. Let alone could I suspect that someday fate would pair us off, and I was going to have to march backward while I did something I'd never intended to do as more than a parlor trick or to amuse children. Remember what I said that first morning we woke up here and Wilshire and LaFarge did their whale-shit riff? That we'd fallen through the looking glass? Well I never thought we'd fall so far through it that all you could see in any direction would be a warped, fun-house reflection of what you'd always thought was the real and solid world."

For their final three weeks of basic training, Leon, marching backward and facing the rest of the platoon, provided nearly all the cadence to and from their training in self-treatment for wounds and squad patrol tactics and VD prevention—a class Peter remembered chiefly for a single line of advice from their instructor: "If she tells you 'no shoes, no shoes' before you dip your wick, you tell her, "uh-uh, baby. I'm gonna wear TWO shoes!'" Wilshire, who earlier in their training had delegated most drill and march duties to LaFarge, now constantly marched at Leon's elbow. It seemed to Peter that Wilshire often leaned slightly toward Leon, as if he heard something in his humming and glottal clucking that drew his concern.

Wilshire had Leon stick with the Bach two-part inventions for a couple of days. When the platoon passed other marching platoons, Peter watched with satisfaction as those formations fell into disarray as complete as if they'd been struck by a sonic torpedo, the men swiveling their heads to gawk at Leon, the sergeants bawling commands to get back in step and darting angry, puzzled glances at Leon and Wilshire. Yet Wilshire looked more and more dissatisfied as he watched from his backward-marching perspective the men keep step in complete silence. Peter puzzled over the incongruence between Leon's growing mastery of what Wilshire had asked of him and what looked like Wilshire's deepening displeasure with it until, on the second day, the answer popped into his head. The music Leon was whistling and humming and the march-time he was setting with plucked vocal cords wouldn't work long-term as cadence because it offered platoon members no way to participate.

At sunset on that second day, Leon and Wilshire set out on another backward march together around the same block of barracks they had used for their first dry run. This time Peter stood on the landing and listened until they were out of hearing range. He could tell they were testing marches that could be broken into two distinct parts, one for Leon and one for the rest of the platoon. When Wilshire and Leon rounded the final corner and headed back up the street toward the barracks, Peter knew they'd nailed it. Wilshire faced forward, but he had fallen back to roughly where the first rank of platoon members would march. He was whistling the march the British prisoners had whistled in the film *The Bridge on the River Kwai,* the "Colonel Bogey March." Leon supplied the march's bass line through the megaphone by humming and doing whatever he did that made his vocal cords vibrate like the plucked strings of a bass viol.

That began what Peter remembered as the late, golden period when mastering the music they marched to was the platoon's most demanding task and its highest aspiration. Part of Wilshire's incentive in picking the "Colonel Bogey March," Peter concluded, was to ease the strain on Leon and preserve his vocal fitness for the end-of-training, pass-in-review before the training brigade commander. And a performance of dazzling novelty at that event, Peter believed, was Wilshire's heart's desire.

At the end of the first week of Leon's cadence-setting duty, Wilshire stalked down the aisle between the bunks during what was ordinarily the recruits' single free hour before Taps and lights-out. He was carrying a tall paper cup. He faced about in front of Leon's footlocker and glared down at him, and Leon wearily drew himself to attention.

"You will drink this," Wilshire said. "You will drink all of it, and you will do it now. There will not be a single droplet left in the bottom of this cup when you're done. To a microbe down there it will look like the sands of the Sahara, and if he tries to cross it he will die of thirst before he can reach the other side."

Leon drank it down in long swallows, then tapped the cup's rim against his top front teeth to propel any residue through their gap.

"Did you notice I warmed it to the piss-pot temperature I'm sure you love so well?" Wilshire said.

"Yes, drill sergeant," Leon said. "And I know why you did that, drill sergeant. Thank you, drill sergeant."

Wilshire's mouth dropped open and his eyes widened in feigned amazement. "He knows why!" he breathed. "He's just passed the nematode on the long, slow ascent toward actual intelligence! Is it too far-fetched, then, to suppose you might know what you can do on your own with that cup and with these?" He dropped several paper packets into the empty cup and stalked away down the middle aisle, stopping briefly to berate Simpson for having his shoes misaligned beneath his bunk.

Leon fished the packets out of the cup. They were salt. "He means I should gargle with warm salt water," he said. "Those are singers' tricks to protect their vocal cords. They drink warm water instead of cold, and at bedtime they mix warm water with salt and maybe baking soda and gargle with it."

~ * ~

It was mid-September now. Listening to the radio as they were allowed to do in the evenings, Peter concluded the country must have so sickened of the war that newscasters were choosing to omit any mention of it. But he knew that made no difference to the draftees whose names, figuratively speaking, were on the marbles still bouncing around on those thousand roulette wheels that the language school recruiter had talked about—wheels with a certain number of slots that would serve as chutes into body bags. As the end of their training drew nearer, it seemed to Peter that a cloud of anxiety stole in through the barracks' window screens and settled around those men, most of them several years younger than himself, who foresaw they might tumble into one of those slots. That cloud conferred on them a dignity the others honored in ways large and small.

No one on the floor said anything when Anthony Wilder continued reading a letter from his father by a battery-powered lamp clipped to his bed frame after LaFarge had given the "lights out" call up the stairwell and thrown the switch. Everyone on the floor knew Anthony's father was jailed and awaiting trial, because Anthony was like a broken record on his own narrow avoidance of the same fate. He had worked for his father in the family business, an automobile chop shop in Galax, Virginia, until he was drafted. Two weeks after he arrived at Fort Bragg, the police had raided the chop shop and arrested his father and Anthony's first cousin. Given this recent trauma and the growing understanding that certain draftees, Anthony among them, had the mark of combat arms upon them almost like the mark of Cain, no one on the floor was going to tell Anthony to switch off his light, despite the likely consequences, which swiftly came to pass.

After he gave the "lights out" call, LaFarge had walked around the outside of the barracks and seen the light through a window. The infraction netted the whole second floor an extra six-hour shift of KP. When LaFarge stormed up the stairs to tell them that, he said he wasn't even going to ask who'd had his light on, since it was everyone's duty to see that an order to the group at large was promptly obeyed. No one told LaFarge whose light it was. And so far as Peter knew, no one complained to Anthony about it, either.

Simpson felt the mark on his own brow, and perhaps because of it, he seemed intent on shriving himself with Leon, though he still would not concede his point regarding Leon's sexuality. Not long after the match with pugil sticks had forged a sort of bond between himself and Leon, Simpson had told Leon and Peter they could call him Pen. When Peter asked him if that was short for something, Simpson dropped one foot backward in a stance suggestive of a small dog guarding a bone, and he said his full name was Pender Perquimans Simpson. Peter said that sounded like a name of distinction. Simpson said Pender was the name of his mother's home county, where she still went to pick cotton every fall. Perquimans, he said, was the county where his parents had their own small farm and grew burley tobacco for market and the peanuts they sold at a roadside stand.

A few days after Wilshire installed Leon as the setter of cadence, Simpson came down the aisle in that hour before lights-out and told Leon sheepishly that not only was he starting to kind of like the music Leon made, but he preferred it by far to the mostly vulgar lyrics of the cadence chants used by drill sergeants base-wide.

"But just so you understand—see, I never knew any Black person who made sounds with his mouth like the ones you make that wasn't queer."

"Pen, did you ever know any white person that could make music the way I do?" Leon said.

"Hell, no! I never knew anybody that made music the weird way you make it."

"Did you ever know anybody that you knew to be what you are calling queer?"

Simpson snickered a little. "Anybody who really was queer would know better than to act that way around me. If he tried it, he'd be mighty sorry."

"I see," Leon said. "Well, if you've never known anybody who can make music the way Sergeant Wilshire has me making it, and you've never met anybody you knew to be queer, then how can you know that only queers are likely to make music that way?"

Simpson was clearly prepared for that one.

"Because my church teaches me that those who love the Lord are empowered to detect the works of Satan," he said.

Leon's head slowly tilted forward and his eyes widened until the whites in them resembled the enormous eye-whites of a character trapped in a darkened room in a movie cartoon.

"And do you love the Lord, Pen?" Leon said. "Do you truly love the Lord?"

Simpson squared his shoulders and did a little bantam strut.

"You bet your Black ass I love the Lord!" he said. "I know that my Redeemer liveth!"

What Peter remembered best from listening to the radio in those waning days of summer was how all conversation would shut down abruptly each time a DJ in Fayetteville plopped a vinyl disc on a turntable and the sweet, two-note opening of Paul McCartney's plea to Jude welled from the transistor sets propped on footlockers and against pillows. And he remembered how the silence throughout the barracks remained complete until McCartney's voice rose, repeating at rising pitch and volume his one-word prediction of improvement for the lovelorn Jude, and how by the time McCartney got to the single syllable that dominates the song's final lines, it seemed everyone on both floors of the barracks was singing those nonsense sounds that, at least while they were singing them, made more sense to them than anything else in their lives.

Leon gargled nightly with warm salt water. As the platoon entered its final week of basic training, it seemed to Peter that Leon's voice was holding up fine, but each night Leon collapsed with exhaustion on his bunk after marching backward all day.

"Why won't he let you switch around and lead cadence from the rear of the platoon?" Peter asked. "You'd be marching forward then, and with the megaphone, everybody could still hear you fine. Is it just that he figures that shouldn't happen down on the old plantation?"

"This pass-in-review in front of the brigade commander—that's what all this is aimed at," Leon said wearily. "Wilshire wants this guy to experience a certain frisson when we march past him, and he thinks it will take a delicate mix to achieve that. And apparently that mix has to include somebody as Black as me leading cadence and marching backward."

As abusive as the demands on Leon seemed, Peter felt the final few days of drill proved a blessed diversion for those platoon members who feared the Jolly Green Giant that Wilshire so liked to conjure would send them to places where the governing cadence was the rat-a-tat-tat of small arms, interrupted by the occasional cymbal-crash of incoming rockets. Instead of dwelling on that likelihood while marching to mindless Jody chants, they were straining in well-nigh joyous concert to master intricacies of counterpoint. Marching constantly beside Leon, sometimes marching backward as well so that he could observe the rest of the platoon, Wilshire donned the Zen-like persona that had heretofore appeared only on the firing range. Timing his comments for intervals of silence in the "Colonel Bogey" and another march they had adopted, "The British Grenadiers," Wilshire would say things like "that's good, that's good" and "now you're getting it" in a voice just loud enough to carry the length of the column. During an extra two hours on the drill field on their last day before graduation, Peter, marching midway down the column, thought he saw in Wilshire's hangdog face a glimmer of the same exaltation that Leon's amplified vocal acrobatics and their own whistling evoked in the rest of them. And Peter thought that, however ulterior his motive, Wilshire had given them something that any soldier should treasure if he was lucky enough to have ever had it. Wilshire had given them a time unlike any other, a time out of time, when their hearts were high and their fears fell by the roadside like discarded gear that could only hamper their advance through the battle-smoke. After all, Peter thought, by improvising with what came to hand—Leon's freakish talent—Wilshire had made passable soldiers of them all, and in doing so had proved his own worth. Before he dismissed the platoon, Wilshire told them fall into two ranks and come to attention at the foot of the barracks steps. He stalked along each rank, glaring into each man's face but saying nothing.

"I was looking for some hint of military fitness in your faces just now," he said finally, facing both ranks and shaking his head. "Makes about as much sense as searching for broncos on a worm ranch. Nonetheless, tomorrow every sad and simple one of you will receive the rank of private. To adapt a phrase often invoked by my fellow Texan, Lyndon Johnson, God help the United States of America.

"Now listen up. At O nine-thirty hours, we will form up here and march to the drill field. At ten hundred hours all four platoons that finish basic on this training cycle will pass in review before the brigade commander. We will then return to the barracks in formation, and you will form up again here just as you are now, and I will then hand each of you a small plastic packet containing your chevrons. If I were allowed, I would wear a poncho when I hand those out, since big green tears are likely to rain down at the sight. You will remain in formation while I will read to you your advanced training assignments. You will then be dismissed for chow. After you return to quarters, I will offer you what those of you who possess some trace of intelligence might count as a rare opportunity. Questions?"

Leon, still facing the rest of the platoon, leaned a little toward Wilshire and said something in a voice too low for Peter to hear. Wilshire nodded curtly but said nothing.

"Anyone else?" Wilshire said. "Good. Meriwether, you stand at ease. The rest of you are dismissed."

Whatever Leon had to say to Wilshire took only a couple of minutes. Peter had just sat down on his locker when he saw Leon step through the far door with a look on his face that brought to Peter's mind all he had heard about the thousand-yard stare. Leon slowly lowered himself to his footlocker, still without looking at Peter or anyone else. He removed his boots and slumped forward with his eyes closed and palms folded. He remained like that, motionless, while Peter stripped to his skivvies and took his transistor radio out of his locker. Rather than switch the radio on, he studied Leon's face, wondering if he was praying or asleep. "Leon?" he said softly.

Leon reacted as if to a starting gun. He launched into the first hambone routine he had attempted since his cadence-setting duties began three weeks earlier. He kept at it until men from the first floor began crowding the doorways at either end of the rows of bunks. All the men were bone-weary, and even though a few of them clapped with a semblance of their old delight, others seemed indifferent or resentful. Leon slapped his legs, chest, arms, shoulders and cheeks at ever-accelerating speed, until Peter realized with alarm that Leon had overstepped the desire to entertain and was veering toward uncontrolled frenzy. "Leon, enough!' Peter said. Leon, eyes shut, seemed to hear nothing but whatever wild Dionysian rhythm coursed through his brain. Finally, Peter wrapped his arms around Leon's arms below the shoulders. "That's enough, Leon!" he said. "Enough, enough!"

~ * ~

At lights-out, LaFarge said they could keep their radios on for a half-hour. Peter propped his beside his pillow, hoping to hear McCartney make his gentle plea once more before he had to shut it off. Then he heard Leon grinding his teeth in the upper bunk next to his own. Leon started to mutter in his sleep, and Peter leaned over the edge of his bunk to hear better.

"Just have 'em mark time," Leon said. "Mark time, mark time, and I'll make it happen. Then we can go. We can all—just—go."

When they formed up outside the barracks next morning, Wilshire and LaFarge wore pressed uniforms. Wilshire's triple-wrapped laces looked more than ever like a tightly constricting band atop each gleaming black combat boot.

"Listen up," Wilshire said. "I harbor no illusion about your individual or collective fitness to adapt to a change in plan. But now that you are about to pass from under my tender tutelage, I perhaps owe you a chance to prove me wrong. As step one in this proof, I will ask you to execute a simple command without stepping on your dick."

Wilshire gave the command "mark time, mark!" and the platoon members, all in ranks except for Leon, who stood facing them, marched in place in time to Wilshire's "hut, hut, hut." Then Wilshire called halt and reminded them they would be the last of the four platoons to circle the drill field, winding up with a pass-in-review before the brigade commander. They would whistle the "Colonel Bogey March" for their full circuit, while Leon, marching backward and facing them, set cadence in his special way.

"Now listen up and listen good!" Wilshire said. He told them that when they reached the reviewing stand, he would give the mark time command. "And you will mark time in *complete silence!*" Wilshire and LaFarge then split the chore of stalking through the ranks and barking into each platoon member's face, Leon excepted, the question "how will you mark time?" and getting from each the only acceptable answer, "in complete silence, drill sergeant!" Peter was in Wilshire's sector, and when Wilshire leaned in close to snarl his question, Peter glimpsed the shadowed depths below the pouched eyelids. For an instant he felt giddy, sensing there was nothing down there. During the rest of the man-by-man interrogation, Peter tried to catch Leon's eye, hoping Leon could lip-read the question "What's this about?" and provide some lip-readable answer. But Leon stared stonily straight ahead.

They marched to the drill field in silence, save for a barely audible "hut, hut, hut" from Wilshire, who marched at one side of the formation. Leon led the formation, marching forward like everyone else to save energy. Something's just not right, Peter kept thinking, but he could find no focus for his rising dread, except that it had to do with Leon.

The first thing that struck him when they came in sight of the field was the absurd height of the reviewing stand. He had expected a platform taller than the one where they had fought with pugil sticks, certainly, but not a monstrosity high enough to induce vertigo. He assumed the stand's ground-length blue draping must conceal a wheeled frame, and the kind of wheeled staircase used to board an airliner stood at one end of the platform. There appeared to be room atop it for a whole Bob Hope USO show, complete with a troupe of Rockettes, but instead just five figures—reduced to doll-like proportions by their elevation, distance and isolation on that mammoth stage— stood at attention center stage, above a garish, shield-shaped insignia on the draping. The hat brim of the officer in the middle threw off flecks of sunlight like a Lilliputian fireworks display. Peter knew that one must be the brigade commander, since only a general's hat brim would be festooned with what looked like gold-colored, symmetrically arrayed bird poop.

A running track surrounded the drill field. The first three graduating platoons circled the track to the kind of Jody chants that had served generations of drill instructors and recruits. But these platoons were using none of the obscene chants that, to Peter's mind, at least had the saving grace of imaginative flair. Throughout his weeks of training, Peter had noticed that when his platoon crossed paths with others, drill sergeants were winnowing the foul language from their cadence counts. Only lately had LaFarge confirmed the reason. Pressure had passed down through the chain of command, even though anyone who had ever been a field commander would know the folly of asking military culture to purge itself of language that springs from it as naturally as day lilies from a dung heap. Into this mix of obscene chants, Leon was about to introduce the "Colonel Bogey," something that, given this pressure to bowdlerize, the commander of the training brigade would be sure to approve.

In their final days of drill, Leon had inserted yet another virtuoso element in the platoon's performance of the march. In its first one-third, he limited his contribution to viola-like plucking sounds from his vocal cords. Then he would shift to humming that mimicked the trombone slides in the march's minor-key middle section. When the march shifted back to major in its final third, Leon picked up the bass line with glottal plucking, as he had been doing since he and Wilshire first chose the march. But now, by whistling with clarinet-like resonance through the gap in his front teeth, in tones at least a full register below the shrill, fife-like whistling from the rest of the platoon, Leon also added a middle line of counterpoint that completed the likeness to the full "Colonel Bogey."

Wilshire, standing to one side of the column, waited until the last of the preceding platoons neared the end of the track's straightaway. Clearly he wanted there to be no inane cadence-chant competing for the commander's ear by the time his platoon reached the reviewing stand. During the previous day's drill, Wilshire had calculated the distance they would cover on the track while performing the "Colonel Bogey." To make sure Leon didn't veer from the proper route, he had even chalked a lane for Leon to follow. Today, he had positioned them where they would end up in front of the reviewing stand when they whistled the last notes of the march. Peter thought: So that's where we'll mark time. And what happens then? As Peter watched the platoon ahead of them enter the far turn and the sound of their chant faded in his ears, suddenly a carping voice piped up in his brain. "Wouldn't he like to get a second rocker below those chevrons out of this?" the voice asked. "Wouldn't he now?"

"For-waaard—march," Wilshire said, just loud enough for them all to hear. Leon led the platoon by himself, marching backward as usual, while Wilshire and LaFarge kept pace halfway down the column on either side. To Peter, once the marching and whistling started, it all seemed indistinguishable from all the other times they had drilled the "Colonel Bogey"—a half-dozen times yesterday alone, on this same stretch of track—except that the voice in his brain was now pleading with Leon: Don't do it. Whatever it is, that extra thing he's asked you to do, it's too much. My God, haven't you've done enough?

By the time they reached the turn at the end of the track's straightaway, Peter could see that the platoon ahead of them had cleared the reviewing stand and was headed toward the track's far end, where the other two platoons, still in close-order formation, had marched off toward their barracks. Coming out of the turn, Peter and the others launched into the final third of the "Colonel Bogey," and Leon, hewing to a plan worked out during the previous day's drill, dialed the megaphone to top volume with his thumb and deployed the full range of his vocal and whistling powers. Peter could tell the chalk lines had served their purpose. Leon's eyes merely flicked downward a few times to note where the lines were, but he hadn't moved his head at all. It's all working out as we drilled for it to do, Peter thought, as they entered the shadow of the giant reviewing platform. And now what? And where's that chill coming from? Christ, it's still September. Why that sudden chill?

"Pla-toon, halt!" Wilshire said. "Mark time—mark!" Then more softly: "By my count, men. Hut—hut—hut." It was much slower than their marching cadence. Leon had lowered the megaphone. His feet didn't move, but his head bobbed slightly as he absorbed the cadence. Then he lifted the megaphone again and, with that mix of hummed notes and plucked vocal cords, he launched into a series of arpeggios that Peter recognized as a simple Bach prelude. As the arpeggios went on and on, Peter almost laughed in relief, thinking: Is that all it is? What's that supposed to accomplish? Well, what harm can it do?

But then Leon started whistling through the gap in his teeth in that impossibly low register that sounded so like a cello. The first whistled note lasted as long as two of the arpeggios that were coming from his throat, and the second whistled note spanned another two arpeggios, and Peter thought: God, how does he find the breath for this? Wilshire was almost whispering now: "Hut—hut—hut." Then Leon whistled a quick bridge to a higher note, and suddenly Peter knew what this was. For whatever advantage Wilshire sought to gain with that rigid figure standing twelve feet above ground and wearing a hat adorned with golden bird shit, Leon was performing the 'Ave Maria' that Gounod had overlaid on a Bach prelude.

"Hut—hut—hut," Wilshire said softly, and Peter whispered through clenched teeth, "So your stock rises, does it, once you've pawned him off as your trained monkey?" But then Peter's fury at Wilshire ebbed as Leon's whistling soared so high above those arpeggios that he kept plucking from his throat that it seemed impossible both could come from just one body with just one set of lungs. Now what the hell? Peter thought, raging at himself as he listened to the tender descent from that crescendo toward the closing amen. What in the goddamned fucking hell? he thought, unable to wipe his stinging eyes. This is just Leon whoring himself to buy that rocker for Wilshire—God knows why he should. So why these goddamned tears?

"Platoon—halt!" Wilshire called when Leon's final, drawn-out whistle had died away. Leon switched off the megaphone with his thumb and lowered it to his side. He stood at attention with his chest heaving and a little rivulet of sweat running down either side of his flared nostrils. All of them, even Wilshire and LaFarge, stood silently at attention until Peter wondered what they were waiting for. Then he heard a clatter of footsteps and realized someone was descending the stairs at the end of the platform. An officer wearing khakis with a major's golden oak leaf on his collar stepped up to Wilshire, and they exchanged salutes.

"General Hanrahan asked me to deliver his compliments on the platoon's performance," the officer said. "He also asks that the platoon's ranking NCO and the recruit who was out front with the bullhorn and who did that—I'm not sure what to call what he did, except to say it was amazing. The general asks that those two men come up to speak with him briefly."

Wilshire ordered the platoon to stand at ease and he and Leon followed the major up the stairs. The stand-at-ease order didn't allow for gawking, but Peter could tell that would be useless anyway. He was standing too close to the blue draping to see what was happening on the platform above him. After a few minutes, Wilshire clattered back down the rollaway stairs. Leon climbed down behind him, but much more slowly. He looked, to Peter's eye, as if he'd been poleaxed. Wilshire's face told Peter nothing.

They marched back to their barracks. Instead of leading the platoon, Leon fell into the front rank. Wilshire called a simple "hut, hut" cadence. From his spot near the middle of the formation, Peter couldn't get another look at Leon's face. When they reached the barracks, they fell out of marching formation and formed two ranks, and Peter elbowed his way to a spot next to Leon. Wilshire went inside to fetch the chevrons from his tiny office on the second floor.

Leon looked straight ahead, squinting a little, as if he were trying to make out something in the distance.

"What did they do to you up there?" Peter said.

"Nothing," Leon said. "The general said he liked what we'd done. He asked us whose idea it was, and I said Sergeant Wilshire and I worked it out. He asked what was that last piece I did, while we were marking time, and I told him it was the 'Ave Maria'. He thought that over for a little bit, and then he said, 'Sacred music, huh? Well, they want 'em clean, and you can't get 'em any cleaner than that.' He said personally he thought cleaning up the cadence counts was a lame nag of an idea, but we'd made it gallop like a thoroughbred, and he'd like to hang onto men who could do that. He seemed to know Sergeant Wilshire pretty well. He told him he thought it was time he got a bump in rank, and he'd see what he could do about that."

"Wait, wait, wait," Peter said. "He said he'd like to hang onto you? What was that supposed to mean?"

"I don't know. Maybe nothing. Nothing bad, for sure. Wilshire said the same thing, by the way," Leon said, and for a few moments his eyes were fixed in that thousand-yard stare. "Yesterday, after I asked him about adding the 'Ave Maria', he said if it was up to him he'd put me on rewind, and when he gets his next basic training platoon in two weeks, we'd do it all over again. He said he just wanted me to know that."

"Well, that explains the way you looked when you came up the stairs in the barracks last night, and the way you look right now."

"Yeah? How's that?'

"Like you'd been zapped with a stun gun and were about to get hung up on a butcher's hook."

Leon turned toward Peter with a quizzical frown, and his upper lip curled as if he'd bitten a piece of spoiled fruit.

"I look zapped?" Leon said. "Pete, have you taken a good, close look at anybody else's face in this platoon lately? Do you remember what they're about to find out? What Wilshire said about the odds they'll end up in places where the cadence goes rat-a-tat-tat?"

"Well, we're all about to find out what the Army's going to do with us, aren't we?" Peter said.

"Sure, but you and I can do other things the Army needs. You've cut a deal, right? Well, so I have I—if it holds. Look, I know you can't see faces from where you are back in the ranks. But I see them. I've seen them all the time while we drilled these past few weeks, and I got a good look at them out there on the track today. All you saw on my face was the look a man might wear a minute or two after something catches him unawares. It's worse to have to look at a man's face day after day and see the dread creep into it because he knows he might get shipped off to die."

Wilshire came out of the barracks with a paper bag and a clipboard. He and LaFarge divided the small plastic bags the paper bag contained, and they handed one of them, without comment, to each man in the platoon. Each plastic bag contained two cloth chevrons. Most of the men barely glanced at their chevrons before they stuck them in a pocket.

Wilshire circled back to the front of the platoon, shaded his eyes and looked upward. "You people are fortunate beyond belief," he said. "There've been times when I handed out chevrons to a platoon and the giant dropped so many hot green tears they flooded the area and scalded their nuts off, and they all had to reenlist as WACs."

Some new, tacit understanding told the platoon's members they could laugh at this, and they did.

"All right, listen up," Wilshire said. "What I am about to read off are your training assignments as of today—this morning at O nine hundred hours to be exact, when I picked this list up at the training brigade personnel shack." He showed them the typed list by holding the clipboard above his head and slowly turning from side to side.

"Just like a priest," Meriwether whispered to Peter. "That's the way the priest shows off the chalice and host at communion, before he invites the people to come up for a nibble and sip."

"In most but not all cases, training assignments hold firm," Wilshire said. "In most but not all cases, the job you end up doing will be what you have trained to do. With that understood, your training assignments are as follows:

"Atkinson, field artillery; Aubrey, mortuary affairs; Berry, infantry; Blakely, infantry; Casey, ammunition specialist; Dandridge, Defense Language Institute; Daniels, military police; Delahanty, personnel; Espenueva, field artillery; Ewbanks, watercraft operator; Falcone, infantry..."

Shamed by Leon, Peter tried, without success, to imagine what the faces of some of the men must look like as Wilshire read off their training assignments.

"...Jacobi, infantry; Konkle, combat medic; Lee, explosive ordnance disposal; Lisherness, helicopter repair; Lockridge, infantry; Mabrey, field communications; McConnell, infantry; Meriwether, food specialist..."

So maybe nothing bad really did mean nothing bad, Peter thought. Maybe it really can be like Leon was saying in his sleep. Maybe we can all—just—go.

"...Myers, quartermaster; Nicholas, aviation maintenance; Pfeiffer, armor; Pike, OCS; Ramos, infantry; Simpson, infantry; Staples, unit supply..."

Alone among the faces of men who would go for combat, Peter could imagine Pen's face, the mistrustful, neglected child behind the banty-rooster truculence.

"...Taylor, chaplain assistant; Wilder, infantry; Wilson, explosive ordnance disposal; Yarbrough, infantry."

"That's it. Did I skip anyone? All right. Report to the barracks, second floor, at thirteen hundred hours sharp. At that time, I will provide you a little lagniappe to top off these past nine weeks of patient coddling."

Leon went upstairs to his bunk, saying he needed rest more than food. Peter tracked down Pen and Wilder and asked if he could sit with them at chow.

"How do you feel about, you know, drawing the infantry?" he asked them as they set their trays on the table.

Even sitting down, Pen managed to strut. "Counted on it from the first," he said. "I'm here to be a soldier, right? Not a wuss."

Wilder showed none of Pen's elation. "If you get blown away, your family gets that five thousand dollars insurance payment free and clear, right?" Wilder said.

"That's my understanding," Peter said.

"If you don't get blown away, can your family take out a loan against that amount?" Wilder said. "I know you can do that with some kinds of insurance."

"I don't think you can do it with this kind," Peter said. "You get your serviceman's life policy free, so it doesn't have any cash value for you to borrow against."

"So the only way you get anything from it is to get killed?" Wilder said.

"Or die some other way. But you have to be dead."

Wilder frowned and noisily sucked with a straw from his milk carton.

"My dad needs a lawyer," he said. "I thought maybe that insurance plan could help him out."

"Hey, did you know you get extra pay over there?" Pen said. "Infantry gets more pay than anybody, because you're out there in the thick of it. And you can have the Army send your pay straight to your family. Did you know that? Pretty good deal, huh?"

Wilder kept his eyes on his plate. "Better than nothing," he said.

When Peter got back to the barracks, the second floor was filling up with men from both floors, but he didn't see Leon. In a few minutes,

Wilshire came out of his closet-sized office carrying a folding chair. Then Leon stepped from the office, wearing a dialed-down version of the same stunned expression he'd worn when he descended from the reviewing stand, as if whatever he had foreseen then had—no surprise to him—now come to pass. Peter elbowed past several men to get to Leon before Leon reached his own bunk.

"What did he do to you?" Peter hissed at him. "And don't give me that 'nothing bad' crap."

"I'm staying here," Leon said.

"Here? And train for what?"

"No training required," Leon said. "I'll do what I'm already doing. What I've trained myself to do."

"What? But you already got your orders for cook school! Wilshire had it on his list. We all heard it just an hour—"

"Yeah, but that was as of O nine hundred hours, remember? This is as of whenever the general got back to his office and had new orders cut that assign me to the training command."

"Training command? Where? For how long?"

Leon had reached his bunk. Halfway up the ladder to the top bed, he paused, balancing himself with both feet on the little metal rung. Without looking at Peter, Leon spoke as if he were reading from a script:

"I am staying here at Fort Bragg. I will most likely remain here for the rest of my two years in the Army. During all of that time, I expect to work in close concert with Sergeant Wilshire. He and I will, as the colloquial term has it, be joined at the hip." Leon climbed the final two rungs and fell forward onto the mattress.

Peter stood at the foot of Leon's bed. He looked at the floor, and several times he brushed the fingernails of one hand across his cheek. He tried to think the matter through as coolly as if it were a mathematical problem. But that same carping voice in his head that had piped up while they stood in formation on the track that morning was trying to cut in again. It kept getting louder and swept away all the evidence of motive and probability that he was trying to examine. Finally, all he could hear in his mind was: *He got himself that second rocker, didn't he? He got that plus his own personal house nigger. God, what a smart son of a bitch!*

Peter pushed through the men who had crowded around Wilshire until he reached his own bunk. He stood with his back against the bed frame, watching Wilshire, who had unfolded his chair in the middle of the aisle a few feet away.

"It's thirteen O five hours," Wilshire said, loud enough for them all to hear. "Here's the deal. It is generous, I think you will agree, given the nature of our prior relationship. Please note that it is also time-limited. It will expire at fourteen hundred hours. For the next fifty-five minutes, I will answer any question you want to ask, on any topic, truthfully and to the best of my ability. For that time period, the rules of military etiquette won't apply. You can, if you want, pose your question in the manner of one low-life seeking information from another one of the same. Just remember that I'm free to respond like a fellow low-life. So, for example, if you address me as Sergeant Dipshit, I will answer your question to the best of my ability, but I might also beat the crap out of you. So who's first up?"

Someone in the crowd asked what the odds were that an infantryman would get killed in combat.

"It depends on your sector," Wilshire said. "In the Iron Triangle, you probably run a one in ten chance of getting killed or seriously wounded. Elsewhere in-country right now, the odds are probably closer to one in twenty. If you do get wounded, the medevac and field hospital systems have gotten so good that you'll probably survive, though you might carry a colostomy bag for the rest of your life. The really good news is the odds of getting your dick shot off in combat are less than one in a thousand, and unless that happens, you've got something to live for."

Wilder asked his question about borrowing against life insurance. Wilshire simply said, "Won't happen."

"Well, shit," Wilder muttered.

Pike, who as far as Peter knew was the platoon's only college graduate other than Leon and himself, asked why Wilshire wore such long bootlaces that he had to triple-wrap them around the tops of his boots.

"Now, that is an excellent and important question," Wilshire said. "I can see why the selection panel for OCS thought you well suited for the mantle of leadership. If you had ever served as a soldier in the field, you would know how often the need arises for a short length of cord—to tie down a tent flap in a gale, say, or to serve as a tourniquet when you might otherwise bleed to death before a medic can reach you. If you carry a piece of cord in your pack, you might forget it's there, or it may prove inaccessible in a moment of need. But if you wear bootlaces of this length, you can always cut off half of one of them. Even if you use the whole lace, you can still cut the other one in half and have length enough in each half to fasten your boots."

"Are you even real?" Peter blurted. The sound of shuffling of feet on the barracks floor died away. "Are you even fucking real?"

Wilshire's baggy eyelids narrowed a little, but he answered calmly. "I wondered the same thing the first time I took a close look at you and every other recruit in here: Could you even be fucking real? Nine weeks later, I've shaped you into something the Green Giant finds marginally acceptable. I take that as sufficient evidence of my own reality."

"You shaped us?" Peter said, starting to tremble. "You did it? All by yourself, was it?"

"Not entirely. But to an extent you may find it hard to understand, yes."

"I have a question, Sergeant," a man named Yarbrough said. Peter recognized him as one of the recruits Wilshire had patiently coached on the firing range. "I don't want to step out of bounds, but—look, you said we could ask about anything, right?"

"Anything about which I might have actual information," Wilshire said. "If you're wondering how your girlfriend feels about cunnilingus, I can't help you with that."

"Well, I wondered—I know a lot of us wondered—about how you lost your earlobe. I mean, whether you were born that way or something took it off."

Wilshire nodded and leaned back in his folding chair. "That question does predictably come up," he said. "Naturally it's a somewhat sensitive subject for me, but I've worked out a way to respond to it that offers you the truth and provides me with some buffering for feelings left raw by a painful episode in my life. I'll give you two accounts of how I lost that piece of ear. One of those accounts is completely true, though the other may also contain elements of truth.

"The first account is this: I was a young infantryman in the salient at Bastogne in December of nineteen forty-four. We were on what amounted to picket duty, posted in an exposed position, when a German sniper shot off that piece of my ear. It was just luck, of course, that he didn't shoot me through the jugular instead. A fellow named Al Flagler—an infantryman, not a medic—heard me yell that I was hit, and when he saw that a piece of my ear was missing, he looked around for it in the snow. Snow is pretty good camouflage for something as white as a shot-off Caucasian earlobe, and while Al was looking for it, another shot by that sniper dug a furrow in the snow after it narrowly missed Al's head. So he and I beat it out of there and found our lieutenant and told him about the sniper, and then Al took me back to the medical tent, because I was losing a fair amount of blood. The medical officer asked if we had the earlobe, and when Al told him he couldn't find it, the doctor said that was a shame because if he had it he could sew it back on. Al left me there and went back on the line, but he felt really bad about not being able to find the earlobe, and he figured—correctly, as I later learned—that snow would keep an earlobe fresh enough to be sewn back on hours or even a day later. So when it got dark, Al went back out to that exposed position where he'd found me, and he crawled all around in the snow, feeling around in it with his hands for the earlobe. He had to just hope the sniper either wasn't still there or that, if he was, he didn't have a night vision scope. But the sniper must have gone, because Al said nobody shot at him. After a while Al's hands got numb, and he knew there was no point in trying to find an earlobe in the snow with completely numb fingers, so he gave it up. After a couple of days, the medical officer sent me back out on the line, and that's when Al told me how he'd tried again to find the earlobe the night I got shot and how sorry he was he couldn't find it. And I felt so grateful to Al that I kept in touch with him for about ten years, until one of my letters came back marked 'return to sender.' And then some more years went by, and I cross-trained to become a drill sergeant and got assigned to Fort Bragg. And I learned that Al Flagler had left the service and gone to seminary and become music minister at a Presbyterian church in Fayetteville, where he had started a men's choral group called the King's Singers that specialized in music by Telemann and Rameau and Bach. Al let me try out for the group, even though I wasn't in his or any other church, and I found out I had a decent baritone voice. So, as I like to say, you can never know what welcome results might derive, down the curlicued paths of time, from a shot-off earlobe. I owe to this chapter of my personal history a deepened understanding of the role of contingency, the what-if factor, in all of life. For example, what if Al had found my earlobe right after I yelled for help, and what if the medical officer had promptly sewn it back on? I'd have thanked Al, for sure, but I'd probably never even have learned his name. I'd have an intact earlobe to this day, but the King's Singers would lack what I do not blush to describe as a more than passable baritone. A proper understanding of contingency, men, can broaden your understanding of so much in human history. On the other hand, dwelling on it overmuch can drive you nuts.

"Now, there you have version one of why I'm missing that earlobe. Version two is shorter and, frankly, bleaker. That earlobe was bitten off by a stray dog in Cotulla, Texas, when I was two years old. He bit it off, and he swallowed it, in the alley behind my uncle's gas station. My mother dropped me off at the station every morning, and then she went across the street to Woolworth's, where she worked half-days as a cashier. Her brother, my uncle, had a car up on the rack to change the oil and patch a tire when he heard me screaming. He said that by the time he found me behind the garage, the dog was licking my ear and whining and generally acting concerned for my welfare. He said he figured I must have jumped on the dog's back or pulled its tail or something, and it had whirled around and bitten the first piece of me that it encountered, which happened to be my earlobe. Since the earlobe was right there in the dog's mouth and it was warm and tasted pleasantly of blood, the dog went ahead and swallowed it. At least, my uncle figured that's what had happened, since he looked all up and down the alley for the earlobe and couldn't find it. The wound in my ear looked to him like it was clotting up all right, and it was getting on for noon anyway, so my uncle went back to work on the car that was up on the rack, and he was just lowering it when my mother came across from Woolworth's. He told her he had figured it was okay to wait and let her take me to the doctor, since I'd stopped bleeding. She asked him why he'd let me wander out in the alley and he said he didn't have anyone else around the station to help look after me. When she asked if he'd at least shot the dog, he said no, because he figured it wasn't the dog's fault. She quit her job at Woolworth's, and it was years before she spoke to her brother again. Which was a shame. I liked him a lot, and I couldn't fault what he'd done. He was running a garage, not a day care. He could make me laugh whenever he told the story about how the dog ate my earlobe. Anyone else have a question?"

Leaning against his bed frame's metal ladder, Peter felt grateful for the extra support. As he listened to these alternate histories of a missing bit of flesh, there swept over him the same giddiness he had felt when he glimpsed the depths within Wilshire's pouched eyelids. There's nothing down there, he thought. There's nothing beneath all this weirdly lucid language but resounding emptiness.

"Any other questions?" Wilshire said. He checked his watch. "It's thirteen forty-eight hours," he said. "Twelve minutes and that window of opportunity slams shut. You don't want to leave your dick hanging loose on the windowsill, now, when that happens."

Peter envisioned his own better judgment—rendered, he suspected, for all time to come in the image of the woman he loved, Stephanie Ames—raising a warning palm toward him like a traffic cop.

"I have another question, if you don't mind, Sergeant," Peter said.

The puffy eyelids again narrowed slightly. "Lock and load and squeeze off," Wilshire said. "Just remember where the safety is."

"It's a hypothetical, actually," Peter said. "Let's say you had sole charge of some goods, and those goods had a pretty high value, but it took you a while to figure that out. And let's say that once you did figure it out, you gave careful thought to how you might raise that value further—burnish it to a high shine, as it were. And let's say that once you'd worked hard on maximizing that value, the opportunity arose to sell those goods on—oh, I don't know—on the world's tallest auction block. And let's say —speaking hypothetically now—let's say those goods happened to be human, and they just happened to be Black."

Peter felt a sharp tug at his elbow, and then Leon's voice was in his ear, hissing, "Pete, Pete, shut the hell up, man!"

Peter clung with his other hand to the bed frame as Leon tried to pull him away.

"Once you'd marched those goods out in front of that auction block, how do you think you might give them one last tweak to, you know, heighten their appeal to a prospective buyer?" Peter said. "Might you—I don't know—have it or him perform some top-quality minstrel show, right in front of that twelve-foot auction block before you took him or it up there to see whether somebody might bid, I don't know, maybe thirty pieces of silver, or maybe a rocker or something—"

Leon clapped one hand over Peter's mouth, and with his other hand he reached across Peter's shoulders and wrenched free the hand that held the bed frame. Leon pulled Peter away down the aisle toward the stairwell, and the crowd of men peeled apart to make room for Leon's rescue effort. Just before the alley created by their parting closed again, Peter saw Wilshire still sitting calmly in the folding chair. His head topped with the Smokey Bear hat was tilted just enough to indicate mild interest.

"He doesn't understand, Sarge!" Leon shouted. "I'll set him straight, okay? He just doesn't know."

Leon kept yanking Peter's arm hard and often enough to keep him stumbling sideways until they reached the rear of the closely packed crowd around Wilshire.

"You fuck up my goddamned knee, Leon, and so help me, I'll punch your face!" Peter said. Leon quit pulling but he grabbed Peter by both shoulders and swung him around to face him.

"If you don't want your knee fucked up, then quit fucking with my next two years!" Leon said. "Now listen to me. You think that 'Ave Maria' this morning was Wilshire's idea? It was my idea. I asked him last night if I could add it in, and if that could be the last piece, so that I'd get to do it right in front of the reviewing stand."

"Oh, and I bet he had no problem with that, did he?" Peter said. "It was your idea, was it? Kind of like doing that Bach piece in the hospital was your idea, and all Wilshire did was just give you your head after that, and you ended up marching backward for three weeks and gargling with warm salt water so your vocal cords wouldn't snap like frayed catgut. But it was all really your idea, so that was fine. And then when you had another splendid idea, all Wilshire did was go along with that, and you end up getting screwed out of the one good thing you hoped the Army might do for you while he gets his second rocker. But that's fine, too, because it was all really your idea."

Leon kept shaking his head while Peter was talking. "You don't understand, Pete," he said. "Wilshire had no more to do with my asking to do the 'Ave Maria' than he did with my piping up the day they Gatling-gunned our arms in the hospital. I didn't do either one for Wilshire. I did them for us. Maybe that 'Ave Maria' will mean something someday to the ones like Pen and Ramos and Wilder if they run into some really bad stuff. If I'd known from the first that Wilshire was going to turn any of what I wanted to do to his advantage, I'd have told him to go ahead. I'd have said—hell, I do say—that he deserves that."

"So being joined at the hip to Wilshire, that's hunky-dory with you, too?" Peter said.

"I hadn't counted on that part," Leon said quickly. "Yeah, he gives me the creeps, just like he does you. I've worked with him long enough now to know what to expect. It's like working with a really complicated, really profane windup toy that's all just mechanism, nothing human in there. But look: What good would it do me to go to Army cook school or work in a chow hall? I'm way past learning anything useful from that. And if I did go to cook school, who knows where I'd be sent next? Could be Vietnam, could be anywhere. This way, I stay close to home.

Maybe I can find a place to live off-base with my wife and my little boy. Maybe I can get on part-time at a restaurant in Pinehurst or Southern Pines. In late fall, early spring, golfers from places like New York and Boston come down to play the courses there. Maybe I could convince a chef I could help up his game with golfers who have high-end dining standards. So there's a lot to like about getting stuck here at Bragg. You want me to blame Wilshire? The more I think on it, I figure I owe Wilshire."

"So. All right. But look—" Peter tried to find a way to say it without sounding dumb or condescending. "Look. Doesn't it bother you at all that—remember when you said that if you asked them to make you an Army musician, some white band leader would look at your face and think, 'here's our Nat King Cole look-alike for officers' club dances!' And then you'd feel miserable, knowing you'd chosen that?"

"Yeah, yeah, and I still think that," Leon said. "But the key word there is 'chosen.' If I'd written down 'musician' on the wish list they let us hand in, I'd have seen that one word pointing like a compass needle to two years of me up in front of all-white crowds at ROTC balls and such. I'd be putting on a kind of Blackface performance while, conveniently for the Army, I happened to wear a real Black face. You watched *Amos 'n' Andy* on TV when you were growing up, didn't you? So you see, it's just fine to caricature Black people as long as you have real Black people doing the caricature."

"And what this general wants you to do here, that's way different?" Peter said. "I don't see it."

Leon laughed, three descending musical notes. "Oh, but it is, it is!" he said. "It all lies in that key word, 'chosen.' If I'd said I wanted to be an Army musician, then I'd be choosing what that compass needle was pointing to. Remember back when I said we'd stepped through the looking glass, and we needed to look for ways to enjoy life on this side of it? Well, there were just two ways I could help make that happen, and cooking wasn't an option—not while we were in basic training, I mean—so I tried the other one, which was music. I had no idea what I did in the hospital that day would get me stuck marching backward and whistling into a megaphone. No way could I have foreseen that.

I was just trying to make the point that, no matter which side of the looking glass we were on, we weren't whale shit. Same thing with what I did out there today. I thought I could remind everybody that they were the complete opposite of whale shit. The 'Colonel Bogey' doesn't quite do that, but the 'Ave Maria' sure does. That's all I was trying to do. That's all that the choices I made were about. If Wilshire or that general makes something else out of them, that's their doing, not mine."

"And it's okay if you let them get away with it, is it?" Peter said. "Even knowing it's a kind of minstrel show they're forcing you into? Of course, the Army being the Army, I don't know what you could do about it anyway."

"Well, yeah," Leon said. "Probably nothing I could do." Then he looked up toward the barracks' rafters and said nothing for a while. "A long time ago, my granddaddy, my mother's daddy, told me there weren't but two things I had to do in life," he said. "He'd lived his whole life in Wilmington, see, and he remembered the race riot there back when he was a kid. He told me the old saw about death and taxes had it wrong, because if you have a good enough accountant, taxes are optional. But he said I do have to die someday, and until then I do have to be Black. You were an athlete, right? So let's say being Black is the sidelines. I try to play the game the best I can within the sidelines. About an hour ago, I found out the sidelines had gotten really narrow. I can still see several plays ahead that I can make, though, and they might turn out to be good plays. I can live with that."

The crowd clustered around Wilshire was breaking up. Peter and Leon stepped between two bunk beds as men jostled past them in the aisle. When it seemed to Peter that the men headed back to the first floor had all passed, he started to step backward into the aisle, but before he had completed his step, what felt like an elbow jabbed him hard in the small of his back. He stumbled forward and his mouth struck the foot rail of an upper bunk. At first he was only aware of the bitter taste of metal. He dry-spat a couple of times, trying to clear that taste from his tongue. Then he tasted blood.

"Private Dandridge!" Wilshire's voice said. "Fancy meeting you here! Last I saw of you, it looked like your handler was dragging you out of a lane of traffic. Now here you are, stepping right out into traffic again."

Peter turned, a little woozily, wiping his fingertips across his mouth and seeing the blood on them and starting to feel a deep pain in the left side of his lower lip. Even before he saw how Wilshire had bellied up close to him the way he did to recruits on their first day of basic, Peter felt suddenly glad that Wilshire had clarified matters that were getting muddled in his mind.

"You sorry son of a bitch," Peter said, pressing his hand against his mouth.

"O-ooh, ill-advised language!" Wilshire said, leaning in still closer. "But fortunately for you, spoken in pain and in haste." Without removing his eyes from Peter's face, Wilshire whipped out a handkerchief and held it in front of Peter's mouth. Peter took it and pressed it to his lip, saying nothing.

"You might want to get that cut looked at," Wilshire said. "Unfortunate thing to happen on our last day together. Unfortunate, too, that you left the area when you did. I had an answer to your question all ready to deliver. And, sorry, but that time window has now closed. And, oh my, it looks like it clipped your lip on the way down."

"Yeth, thath jutht too bad," Peer said through the handkerchief.

"In consideration of your current condition, I will give you a partial answer," Wilshire said. "Partial, but I think sufficient. When I look at Meriwether or you or any other recruit, I don't see Black or white or red or yellow. All I see is Army green."

"Thath the one thing I never thought to thee or hear fron you," Peter said through the handkerchief. "Trite. You thaid thonthing trite."

Wilshire looked at him a moment longer. Peter saw in his face neither anger nor amusement nor satisfaction nor anything else except the emptiness within the sagging flesh below the eyes. Then Wilshire turned away. Peter heard his feet descending the stairwell.

He turned toward Leon. "Thankth for your thupport," Peter said.

"You ought to get that cut looked at," Leon said. "He was right about that."

"Yeah? What elth wath he right athout?" Peter said.

"Look, you want me to say he hit you on purpose?" Leon said. "I couldn't see that from here. I saw you step back, and then, wham, your mouth hit the bed, and then Wilshire was there."

"Yeah?" Peter said. "Well, I thee one thing clearly."

"What's that?"

"Joined at the hit."

"What?"

"At the *goddanned hit!*" Peter said through the handkerchief, slapping his own hip.

Leon rolled his eyes. "Come on," he said. "You're going to the hospital."

They followed a route that the platoon, always marching in formation, had taken often since midsummer. It led down narrow, barracks-lined streets, then along a two-lane avenue. The light, early-fall breeze felt so dry and pleasantly cool when it touched Peter's wound that he trusted it to stop his bleeding, and he merely dabbed at his mouth a few more times to check for fresh blood. He walked beside Leon, neither of them speaking. As they neared the hospital, Peter noticed that a station wagon had pulled to the curb across the street, next to a miniature golf course. He thought the driver must want to offer them a ride. Then he saw that the man pointing at them from the rolled-down window was a scowling major.

"Numb-nuts one and numb-nuts two!" the major bellowed. "You have exactly two seconds to get in formation!" Before Peter fell in behind Leon and fixed his eyes straight ahead, he noticed that a woman sat beside the officer and two children were in the seat behind them. "You will remain in formation and in step until you get to wherever you're headed, if you even know where that is," the major said. "If you're too stupid to understand a rule as simple as that, I suggest you ask your drill sergeant for illustrated instructions on how to wipe your ass." The station wagon pulled forward, but before it left the curb the major pointed back at Leon. "That goes especially for you, Rochester!" he said.

In the emergency room, Peter got two stitches that formed an X across the line between his lower lip and the skin beneath it. The doctor said the stitches should minimize scarring there. When Peter asked if there was anything else he should do, the doctor, a captain, said to ice his lip twice a day. When Peter asked where a barracks rat like him was supposed to get ice, the doctor said he should just try to keep his mouth shut for ten days, when it would be time to take the stitches out.

"Rochester?" Peter said as they walked back, still in single file. Without their new stripes on their sleeves, they were still subject to being treated as basic trainees, as the major had done.

"Jack Benny's manservant," Leon said. "You know, I'd be working on keeping your mouth shut, like the doctor said. I could give you lessons in that."

"Yeah, you do that real well," Peter said. "Except when it sounds like you've got a whole music-making menagerie crammed into the space between your larynx and your tongue-tip."

"That's right. Except when I make music."

"And that never lands you in any trouble, does it?"

"Never in any trouble that doesn't have an upside."

"Yeah, right. You ticked off that list back in the barracks, didn't you? Staying close to home and sautéing mushrooms for fat-assed golfers and all that."

"No, I mean the music. The music itself is the upside, if you do it well enough and somebody needs it."

"What about when the downside includes seeing your buddy's mouth get slammed into a bed rail and his lip split, and all you can do about it is whistle and hum another Bach cantata?"

When they got back to the barracks, LaFarge made his best effort at chewing them out. LaFarge could never strike real fear into recruits. A Howdy Doody smile stayed fixed on his face like a rictus on the face of a corpse. That robbed his threats of much force, even when he made good on them, as he had when he spotted the light from Anthony's bed lamp.

"Where in the damn's hell have you been?" LaFarge bawled at Peter and Leon. Peter said nothing but pointed at his stitches. LaFarge said Wilshire had reported the circumstances of Peter's accidental injury and had directed that Peter go to the brigade orderly room to give his own version. Peter asked if Leon could come with him, since Leon had seen what happened, but LaFarge said Wilshire had ordered Peter to go alone.

"Their workday's done in less than an hour, so you will, repeat will, go immediately if not sooner," LaFarge said. He went up the barracks steps.

"Idle question," Leon said, "but if I'd gone with you, what was I supposed to say?"

"Nothing," Peter said. "I was just hoping you'd make music, since according to you, that never comes amiss."

It was scripted the way Peter expected, so he was able to take care of it quickly. There was a legal affairs officer, a captain, who shoved a copy of Wilshire's account across his desk. Wilshire had said he had accidentally collided with a platoon member who stepped out from between two bunks, and he had advised the private to seek medical care for a split lip.

"That looks right," Peter said. "Where do I sign?"

He went to chow before he returned to the barracks. He had decided, without bothering to consider the justice of it, that he should minimize further contact with Leon, and eating alone was one way to do that. He figured he shouldn't stretch the lip by chewing, so he just ate two ice cream bars, slipping them carefully between his teeth, biting and letting the ice cream melt and slide down. He was swirling the last of the watery coffee in his plastic cup when it occurred to him that if it wasn't precisely because of Leon's race that his and Leon's feelings toward each other had chilled, then it would take some tortured reasoning to explain why not. He wondered what he could do about that.

"Not a damned thing," he muttered.

He took his tray to the metal ledge in a wall of the dining area where the hands of a faceless recruit on KP duty snatched the tray from him. Peter bent down and yelled through the opening above the ledge, "could any of you guys bring me some ice? I'm supposed to ice a cut." Nobody answered, and no ice came. Peter walked back to the barracks.

"All okay?" Leon asked when Peter reached his bunk.

"Yeah," he said. "I made sure nothing more would come of it. And guess what? Without you along to fuck up my route step, I managed to stay in formation."

"Orders came while you were out," Leon said. "I put yours under your pillow so they wouldn't blow off or anything."

The single typed sheet said Peter should report next day to the orderly room for the casual barracks. It said he would remain in casual status pending further orders.

"You?" Peter said.

"Two weeks' home leave," Leon said. "I got a voucher for a bus tomorrow to Wilmington."

All that remained for Peter to do was dump the contents of his footlocker into his duffel bag tomorrow morning and hike to the casual barracks. He ambled along the aisle, giving arm-slaps and handshakes to the men he had gotten to know and muttering his good wishes. He kept reminding himself not to smile and risk popping his stitches. He figured somebody would ask Leon to do a parting hambone, or else Leon would provide one unasked, but that didn't happen.

He found Pen Simpson pacing excitedly beside his bunk. It was less than an hour before lights-out, but Pen was still wearing his fatigue pants and boots.

"I heard that in infantry school, you don't sleep with a stupid rubber duck anymore," Pen said. "I heard that down there, you sleep with the *real thing*! And you keep an ammo clip under your pillow, and they wake you up sometimes in the middle of the night and time you on how fast you can lock and load."

"God have mercy on the man in the bunk next to yours when that happens," said the man in a lower bunk next to Pen's. "Sure as shit, you'll hyperventilate and blow his dick off. Either his or your own."

LaFarge called up the stairs fifteen minutes before lights-out, as he always did. Peter figured he should skip brushing his teeth for a couple of days.

"I'll see you in the morning, won't I?" he asked Leon.

"Sure, if we get up as usual," Leon said. "I'll catch a shuttle to the bus station at eight." Peter heard in Leon's voice a note of wary, un-Leonlike distance.

So that's it, Peter thought as the lights flicked off and he settled back on his pillow. What a sour note to end on.

And then another thought struck him like a chest-high blow with a pugil stick: It was all his fault. If he hadn't put the worst construction possible on what happened at the reviewing stand, and if he hadn't then compounded his error by giving Wilshire a virtual glove-slap in the face in front of the whole platoon, the bond between himself and Leon would have remained intact. And who knows what value they might each have derived from that in after years? Instead, he could figure on a lifetime of mirrored reminders of his folly: a threadlike scar through his lower lip.

"Well, shit," Peter whispered. "Nothing to be done about any of it now. Not a goddamned thing."

"Hey, Leon?" a voice from down the row of beds called. "Leon?"

"What's happening, Bro'?" Leon said. His voice sounded wide awake, and as Leon-like as ever.

"That music you did at the end of the pass-in-review today—that was the 'Ave Maria', wasn't it?"

"Hey, you must be my fellow Catholique, Bro'!" Leon said.

"Yeah. Yeah. I used to hear that in church sometimes. Around Christmas, usually, I think. Well, maybe this isn't the right time of year for it, but—could you sing it, Leon? Could you do that? Sing the words to it, I mean?"

"Hey, man, you sure?" Leon said. "I don't know. It's been a long day for everybody. I don't want to wake people up."

After a few seconds, Peter started hearing the murmured voices from the length of the aisle on either side of his bunk. "We're sure," they said. "We're sure, Leon. Sing it."

Leon took several deep, slow breaths. Peter expected him to climb down and stand in the aisle, but instead Leon merely lifted himself on his elbows and began to sing. Not until he got to the *"Gratia plena"* did Peter remember that, for all the weeks of music that Leon had made for the platoon, they'd heard him sing only once before, way back when they were picking up cigarette butts on their first day of basic. And Peter realized the tenor that had sounded so sweet and clear as it wrapped itself around Otis Redding's lyrics wasn't up to the challenge of Gounod's high notes. Leon's voice rasped on the second *"Sancta Maria."* It broke on the highest note in *"Nobis peccatoribus"* and failed completely at the crest of *"in hora,"* where a breathy whisper took its place. Not until Leon reached the repeated "Amen" at the end did Peter notice a slap-slapping sound. Then he quickly realized that he'd been hearing it all along. Men were lightly slapping their mattresses or the floor beside their beds. They were counting cadence.

When Leon finished, Peter saw shadowed forms at the far end of the barracks, and he heard shuffling feet on the stairs. Men from the lower floor had come up to listen.

"Thanks, Leon," a few voices said. Peter heard a low voice murmuring somewhere to his right, on the far side from Leon. Lifting his head, he could see it was Ramos, who had a lower bed two bunks down from his own. Ramos had both hands on his breast, and his eyes were closed. Peter could make out the beads wrapped around his knuckles and the glint of the metal cross in his fingers.

"Ahora y en la hora de nuestra muerte," Ramos said.

A voice piped up from the far end of the barracks floor. It was Pen.

"Hey Leon, I'm glad your voice was a little off on those high notes," he said.

"Yeah, Pen?" Leon said. "Why's that?"

"Because if you could hit those notes and hold them, that would mean for sure you was a queer."

All was silent for a little while. Then Peter heard Leon chuckling softly.

"Pen, have you ever known anybody, a full-grown man I mean, who could hit those notes and hold them?" Leon said.

"No, I haven't known any full-grown man who could hit those high notes and hold them," Simpson said peevishly. "And no, I've never for sure known a queer, either. But I'll tell you one thing. If I ever did know a full-grown man who could hit those notes and hold them, then for sure he'd be a queer. I do know that much."

Papa-san's Private War

We had it down to a goddamned art before Frackowiak shot Papa-san's water buffalo.

It was 0100 hours and all you could hear was the insects creaking and the frogs hitting the bass strings in the jungle all around the hill the fire base was on. Once in a while you'd hear a monkey's screech and Frack would click off the safety on the fifty caliber, and half a minute later he'd click it back on. I heard a swish-swish and what sounded like a big animal's soft snort, and I flipped up an edge of the tarp next to my hammock. I could see something lumbering around outside the wire where we'd chopped back enough brush to give ourselves a clear field of fire.

Then Frack was firing the .50 caliber, leaning back from it on his heels with his eyes like strobe-lit dinner plates in the tracer glare, screaming, "They're in the wire! They're in the fucking wire!"

Everybody was already out of their hammocks and plastered up against the sandbag wall firing by the time I got the flare gun. Whizz made me keep the flare gun and flares locked inside a metal cartridge box and made me keep the box inside a sort of sandbag shrine on top of his command hooch. So it wouldn't get wet, he said.

I'd gotten Thiel to try to talk some sense into him.

"Sir," Thiel had said, "why the fuck do we have to keep the flares locked and put them way the fuck up there? Why, sir?" Thiel's hair always was as tangled as if lizards had mated in it after lots of foreplay. Whizz stuck his chin up against Thiel's chest and said, "What good are they if they get wet, Sergeant?" Whizz was a runt. Anderson says you see lots of runts in ROTC, at college.

"If you leave the lock off, sir, and let us keep them down here, we promise not to pee in the box," Thiel said. You can drop a locked ammo box in a river and the stuff inside it won't get wet.

"What good are they if they get stolen, Sergeant?" Whizz said.

When you tried to work on Whizz with logic, you always found yourself talking slower and slower, so he could keep up. "Sir, nobody is going to want to steal the flares but the VC, and if there's VC in here, sir, we ain't going to need the fucking flares. Besides that, sir, whoever has to climb up there to get the flares is going to get shot, sir, if there's VC within half a click."

Whizz tried to give Thiel his up-and-down parade ground look. But since Whizz had his chin up against Thiel's chest, he couldn't look any higher than the underside of Thiel's jaw, nor lower than his own jaw. So he gave that up and just smirked at Thiel's breastbone.

"When have you seen VC within half a click of the perimeter, Sergeant?" Whizz said. "Within *two* clicks? Anywhere in the goddamned *area*?"

"Sir, none of us has ever seen any VC around here that we know of, sir," Thiel said, speaking very slowly and using good pronunciation that was easy to follow. "But if there ever was any VC around the perimeter, sir, *that* would be just when we'd need the goddamned flares!"

Whizz's smirk went up an octave, if smirks can do that. "You don't have to worry about that, Sergeant," he said. "Just—don't—you—worry about that. It won't be *you* that has to fetch the flares!"

That was Whizz. We called him Whizz because out on patrol, whenever he wanted to piss, he'd say, "Got to go whizz, troops," and he'd go off into the jungle where we couldn't see him. Thiel would drop down in silent prayer for a punji pit in whatever direction Whizz had picked.

So the flares stayed up on the hooch where Whizz could hear any midnight pilferers crossing the corrugated tin roof, and that was where I fired the flare from that lit up Papa-san's water buffalo draped like a shot-down dirigible over the wire. It had holes as big as footballs in its hide and one horn was shot away. An eye dangled from its socket.

"Albert Simon Frack-a-wak!" Thiel yelled. "Why did you shoot Papa-san's water buffalo, Frack-a-wak? Why, Frack-a-wak? Why?"

Papa-san grew the finest, sweetest grass in Quang Ngai Province, grew it in the shade of the dragon fruit trees on the same hill where his ancestors were buried, fertilized it with contents of a cracked blue china chamber pot that contained not only his own offerings but those too of his wife and his splendidly immodest daughter Ut, who was also our hooch maid. Every day after work, Ut would hoist a tarp she'd rigged up with a pulley, duck behind it, strip off her clothes and bathe in the same banged-up garbage can where she did our laundry. From the tub, she'd croon virginally, "You see, huh? You like, huh? Numbah one cherry girl, huh? You like boom-boom? Hokay, you try boom-boom, Mommy-san *ca cai dau* beaucoup GI!" If one of us was edging up to take a peek, she would make this threat graphic by thrusting a shapely arm around the tarp and scissoring her fingers toward his loins.

And he gave it to us! The sweet little bugger gave us the grass! And Frackowiak had to go and shoot his buffalo.

"I heard something knocking the cans," Frackowiak kept saying when we went outside the wire next morning. The buffalo looked very dead. His tongue was hanging out and his loose eye was on the tongue. Papa-san came up from the village, carrying his plow on his shoulder. He dropped the plow and looked at the buffalo. Then he looked at the plow, and then he looked straight ahead for a while, not at anything. Then he turned around and headed back to the village, leaving the plow. We stood around the buffalo and watched him go.

"What's he gonna' do?" Leonard said. Leonard is Black and he makes loud sucking noises at night. He says that's because he's married. "Is that the end of our grass?" Leonard asked.

"I heard the cans," Frackowiak mumbled. He was trying to balance the loose eye on the toe of his boot and put it back in the socket.

Thiel kicked one of the cans, hard, and the other cans rattled all down the wire. "Hear that?" Thiel said. "Fire, goddamn it! Blow my goddamned foot off!"

"He's declared war," Anderson said later, while we squatted in the shade against the guard post and smoked the last of our grass. Ut had come to work as usual, but she didn't talk to us or look at us. We passed around a joint and watched her shadowed form while she bathed behind the tarp.

"Ut won't be here tomorrow," Anderson said. "You watch."

She wasn't, either, and a little after the time when Ut was supposed to show, Papa-san showed up with a delegation. Three greybeards and a round Chinese in a blue smock. We'd never seen the Chinese before. We learned later he made a livelihood convincing villagers in our sector that he could bargain with Americans. It was a lot later that I learned the blue smock was called a Mao suit, but you couldn't expect grunts like us to know about that.

We'd buried the buffalo and Papa-san stood looking at the mound for a while. Then he went over to where he'd dropped his plow the day before. He circled the plow a couple of times, pointing down at it and talking louder and louder. I guess he was telling the greybeards and the Chinese how important it was, but they must've already known that. The plow was real simple—just a couple of poles and a metal plow point—but Pop and his buff could make it dance. I'd watched them a couple of times when I pulled mid-day guard duty. Halfway down our hill he'd plowed a deep furrow that curved around so it stayed the same height above the paddy. I couldn't figure what that was for until the rains came and enough water spilled out of that furrow to cover maybe an extra half-acre of rice. When the spillover started, Pop came up the hill and poured himself a toast out of a little jug of rice wine. Thiel fetched a fifth of Jim Beam from wherever he had it squirreled away, and he and Anderson and I toasted Papa-san from our side of the perimeter fence. Then all four of us all had a good laugh.

I knew that furrow was still there because Pop warned the graybeards and Chinese to step over it. We tried to get Whizz to let Thiel and Anderson negotiate with them. We told him it would be admitting the business was serious if our officer had to intervene. But nothing doing. The prospect of shining as a tough enforcer with the natives seemed to turn Whizz on. If Pop had just come on his own without bringing the board of aldermen, I think Whizz would've stayed out of it and we'd still be rolling in grass and Ut would still be bathing in our converted garbage can and cheerfully offering to cut our dongs off and Papa-san would still be alive.

Whizz told Applewhite, who was on guard, to keep them clear of the gate. Then Whizz came out of the command hooch strapping on his pistol, to set the proper tone. The round Chinese spoke a language he apparently thought was English, and he finally got it across that 10,000 piastre was a fair settlement for the buffalo. That was about $125 then, before the exchange rate went up.

"Look, Noojen," Whizz said when the Chinese had finished. "Noojen" is not how you say Nguyen and there's no quicker way to piss off a Vietnamese than to say it that way. Plus, this bird was Chinese. If they wear the blue smock, they want you to know they're Chinese. Nguyen is strictly a Vietnamese name, and there's no quicker way to piss off a Chinese than to lump him in with Vietnamese. So, with two words out of his mouth, Whizz had pissed off the whole delegation. Good old Whizz.

"Look, Noojen," Whizz said. "No go. No show. *Di-di mau*. Number ten. *Fini. Bitte?*" Whizz had come to the Nam off a tour in Germany and he spoke international that way.

"The stupid son of a bitch," Anderson said under his breath.

Anderson is what you'd call a dispassionate sort, but he saw what was coming and the rest of us didn't. Papa-san looked Whizz in the eye and started yelling at him in Vietnamese. Then Pop yelled something at the Chinaman and the Chinaman spoke to Whizz again, talking slower and slower and with careful pronunciation in what he thought was English. We sent Thiel out to ask Whizz to let us pay the 10,000 p., but we didn't hope for much. Thiel talked to Whizz like he already knew what Whizz would say, so he wasn't going to work up a sweat at it. Whizz shook his head and Papa-san yelled at him some more. Then Pop waved his arms around and herded the greybeards and the Chinaman away down the hill.

Whizz told us that if you ever knuckle under to an Oriental, you lose face with him forever. He said Pop should have kept the buff penned. Thiel said you could go from Camau to the DMZ and seldom see a buff penned or staked or anything but loose. And besides, he said, where was Pop going to get wire unless he stole it from us? Whizz acted like he hadn't heard that and said his standing firm would immeasurably enhance our standing vis-à-vis the insurgent infrastructure. Presumably, if we couldn't see the logic in that, it was because we were lowly grunts and unable to take the holistic view. Whizz was fond of terms like holistic view and insurgent infrastructure and other gibberish he got out of Field Manual Thirty-Seven Dash Twenty-One. All company grade officers got briefed on that manual when they in-processed down at Camp Conway. Anderson said he knew personally that the author of Thirty-Seven Dash Twenty-One was a female GS-13 who'd never been east of Bermuda or west of Bethesda. He said she'd fractured both elbows and a kneecap while walking her two Afghan hounds on M Street when they bolted after a squirrel. Said she'd been so traumatized that ever since she couldn't write words of less than three syllables.

"It's war," Anderson said. "You watch."

For two days nothing happened except Ut didn't come and our laundry piled up. Then Leonard got desperate and went to raid Papa-san's grass patch and Pop pissed on him.

"He's done ripped that garden to hell and gone," Leonard said when he got back. Leonard had found the patch hoed under and he'd hunted on all fours for some of the plants and Pop had jumped up on one of the little walled-in mounds they put over graves and pissed on him.

"I never seen him till he was leakin' on me, man." Leonard was disgusted. "That ain't no way for the downtrodden races to treat one another," he said.

"Where's Lardbucket?" Applewhite said. Lardbucket was our dog, Applewhite's more than anybody's.

"Don't bother to look for him," Anderson said. That was all he'd say.

In a little while, Ut came up the hill. She didn't look happy. I think she missed us.

"Hey soul buvver he take showah numbah one!"

She held up the little plastic bag she always used to carry her lunch to work. Then she took a piece of meat out of the bag with her chopsticks, waved it at us and ate it.

"Lardbucket!" Applewhite wailed. Then he squatted and rocked back and forth on his heels the way their old women do when somebody in their family has been killed. "Lardbucket," he said. Ut smacked her lips and offered to cut our dongs off and then went away down the hill.

"If we don't pay him now," Anderson said, "he'll turn VC."

"I've seen it happen," Thiel said. Thiel was on his third tour. He said it was the Rabbit God's revenge on him for wearing a rabbit's foot for twenty-three years. He wore a fox's foot for a while after his second tour, he said, to appease the Rabbit God. Now he just wore dog tags. "I'd turn VC myself if I had to keep the silver bars end of that roll of flea shit propped up for more than another five months and eleven days," he said.

People have the wrong idea about the VC. They think the VC is just a bunch of little bitty bastards who run around slinging satchel charges and screaming stuff like "Die in your vomit, imperialist cuttlefish!" But Anderson said the VC is more like a labor union, a Lions Club, a Grange, the Democratic Party and the Molly Maguires all rolled into one. He said people turn VC for all the different reasons that people join almost anything from the Ladies' Aid to the Marines.

"Pop's already VC, whether he knows it or not," Anderson said. "He turned VC when he jumped up on his granddad's tomb and pissed on Leonard." Anderson's jaw was working back and forth, and his eyes were like he was looking somewhere further off than the rest of us could see. "We're gonna' pay him," he said. "Either we pay him or we end up having to kill him. Gimme' your p." All our p. came to a little over 2,000. "He'll have to trust us on that 'til one of us can get down to Conway," he said. "Now the one that's going to tell Whizz had better start limbering up his back muscles so he can kiss it goodbye, because when I find out, I'll save Ut the trouble."

"I'll save *all* you people the trouble," Whizz said, and he stepped out from behind the corner of the closest hooch. Applewhite was supposed to be standing watch, but between mooning over Lardbucket and wanting to hear us better, he'd forgot and wandered closer. Whizz's face was trembling with what looked like a kind of joy. His face was shining almost. He walked up to Anderson and stuck his chin up against Anderson's chest, about level with the name tag and the U.S. Army tag over the pockets. Anderson's shirt was always sopping wet in a big V down his chest, and when Whizz stuck his face up at him, Anderson leaned forward and the shirt flopped down over Whizz's ears.

"Do you have any excuse for your actions, Specialist?" Whizz's voice came out kind of muffled from Anderson's shirt. "Do you have any suggestions as to what measures I should take?"

"Yes, sir!" Anderson said. "You should jump up and kiss my ass, sir!"

Whizz pulled his face out of Anderson's shirt and looked up at him. His face was bright pink and wet all the way back to the ears. He blinked a couple of times, and Anderson was half-smiling the way he always does. When you Indian-wrestle him, it's that half-smile that beats you. Whizz's lower lip dropped and started to quiver, but then he caught himself and the lip snapped back up.

"Would—you—mind—repeating that, Specialist?" Whizz said, baying like a bloodhound.

"No, sir," Anderson said. "Not at all, sir. What I said, sir, was you should jump up and kiss my ass. Of course, you may not be able to do it on the first try, sir. You may have to go into training, sir. I would suggest jogging with weights tied to your ankles, sir, and calf-lifts with a barbell behind your neck. Whatever course of training you select, sir, you must persevere. You must persevere despite the dry heaves, sir. Despite the giddiness that precedes heatstroke. Despite the bits of charred flesh and human hair that stick to your boots, sir. That is the main thing, sir. That is the only thing, sir. You must and you will persevere, sir, because that is the Army way. And the Army way is the only way, sir. That is all, sir."

For a while Whizz just squinted up at Anderson's face like there was something there he wanted to read but couldn't. Then he said, "Sergeant, I want this man confined until I can take him to Camp Conway." And for a while Thiel didn't say anything. Then he said, "I can dig a pit, sir, but we ain't got any pierced steel planking to put over it to keep him from climbing out."

Whizz's face went red again all at once. "You can put him under guard, can't you?" Whizz said. "Do I have to spell everything out before you can comprehend it?"

"No, sir," Thiel said slowly. "I'll guard him. Don't worry, sir, he won't get away."

After Whizz doused the lantern in his command shack, Thiel and Anderson sat up against the sandbag wall of the guard post and took turns with the rifle. Thiel guarded Anderson and then while Thiel slept Anderson guarded himself, ready to nudge Thiel and hand him the rifle if either he or I heard Whizz get up. I was inside the guard post, pulling the midnight to four shift.

Next morning after I turned in, Frackowiak shook me awake. "Papa-san's got a gun," he said. "We seen him running up from the village with it."

When I got to the guard post, Thiel said, "He ran into the jungle. Keep down." All I could see was the branches on the palms and gum trees waving a little in the wind, their leaves still heavy with dew. Then we saw him. He ran out of the jungle catty-corner across the bottom of the hill, through the tall grass, staying low. He was carrying what looked like something out of a museum. Anderson said it was one of the old Chinese rifles that had been passed down from one east Asian revolution to the next since the Taiping Rebellion back in the Manchu

Dynasty. Pop must have scoured the rust off it, because the sun glinted off the barrel as he ran. Whizz was yelling, "Fire! Why don't you fire?" at Leonard in the guard post and Leonard said, "Shit, man, I ain't going to waste the dude just for leakin' on me." Very softly Anderson said, "I'm proud of you, Pop. Your granddad and I are proud."

Whizz ran into the guard post and yanked the fifty-cal away from Leonard. Before he got set to fire, Pop made it into the jungle on the other side of the guard post. Pop must have oiled up that musket, because it worked. Every once in a while, we'd hear a crack like timber breaking, and a little puff of smoke would trail out and maybe a dust spurt would kick up outside the parapet or a hole would open in a sandbag, and Whizz would blaze away. Whizz was having so much fun he didn't bother any more about the rest of us not firing. Pop must have kept that up for a good half-hour. Then there was a longer wait and Anderson took Thiel's rifle and crawled to the back of the compound and Thiel and I followed him. Sure enough, there was Papa-san loping up through the tall grass on the back of the hill, holding his musket by the breech with one hand, zigzagging and bent so low it almost dragged the ground. When he got to where he could get a clear shot at Whizz in the guard stand, he stood up and aimed. He never saw Anderson and Thiel and me. Pop was pretty frail even for a Vietnamese, and his Chinese long tom wobbled all over the place while he tried to aim it. Still, he was close enough to the guard stand that it looked like an even bet he could hit Whizz, who was still hunched over the fifty-cal, his head bobbing back and forth, peering off over the tall grass in the other direction. Anderson said, "Nice try, Pop." Then Anderson shut his eyes and crossed himself, raised his rifle and pulled the trigger. Papa-san's head just exploded.

Everybody came back to the rear wall and looked. Whizz seemed put out because he hadn't gotten to shoot Pop, but he brightened up once he saw what the bullet had done to Pop's head. Anderson got a poncho from our hooch and he and Thiel went toward the gate.

"Where do you people think you're going?" Whizz said.

"We're going to take Papa-san home," Anderson said.

"You're—under—arrest!" Whizz bayed. "You're not going anywhere! And neither is anybody else. The rest of them are just waiting for that."

"The *rest* of them?" Thiel said.

"That's right," Whizz said. "They knew you'd been fraternizing with this one, so they sacrificed him to draw you outside. Remember, these people are fanatics, Sergeant," he said with an air of mystery. "They don't think like we do."

Thiel didn't say anything. It wasn't any use. Whizz ordered Frackowiak, who was our radio humper, to call for support. In a little while a helicopter gunship swept over and shredded some jungle. A troop chopper landed some Marines and they milled around for a while, and when they didn't find anything but Papa-san they got back in the chopper and left.

Whizz was having a great time. He told the Marine captain, "They tried to decoy us with this one. The rest of them were waiting in ambush. Oh, they're cagey, sir. You can't take that away from them. Cagey as hell."

"Could you estimate from the firing how many of them there were?" the captain said.

Whizz thought. "Well, I'd have to be conservative since we really didn't see any of them," he said. "Hell, probably no more than fifty." There was an edge of combat weariness in Whizz's voice. "You never really know how many there are, do you, sir?" Whizz pulled a grim face. "You never know for sure until they're on top of you, and then it's too late." The ravages of bloody clashes beneath the tropical sun lined Whizz's brow and gave his eyes a haunted look. He was having a grand time. He asked the captain to send back some Army MPs from Conway for Anderson.

After the Marines left, Ut and the old woman came up the hill and squatted by Papa-san and rocked on their heels and screamed. The old woman had a blanket. They wrapped Pop in it and carried him off.

"Well, he was a VC," Whizz said happily. "A real VC." Then he went inside the command hooch to write his report.

"But he wasn't a VC," Applewhite said. "He was just pissed off because we shot his water buffalo."

Thiel leaned wearily against the sandbag parapet. His hair looked like a nest of lizards had held an orgy there, then left in a panic.

"Before you draw that distinction for a fucking board of inquiry," he said, "would you mind telling *me* what's the difference?"

Anderson refused commander's punishment under Article 15. Whizz backed off at the idea of a court martial, and I don't blame him. In Whizz's boots, I wouldn't give Anderson a platform and an audience either.

So after a week, Anderson came back. Applewhite called a huddle and told us we ought to frag Whizz while we were on patrol and make it look like an accident. Before Applewhite had finished talking, Anderson shoved him against the sandbag parapet and walked away. Thiel pretended he hadn't heard or seen a thing.

We didn't see Ut anymore, but we heard she'd gotten a job as a meat cutter at the village market. Applewhite said we'd better start sleeping with our pants on and our flies tied to a belt loop. We could tell from his face he was serious.

"We'd better find him another dog," Anderson said.

A Valley of Dead Marines

I can almost always pick them out now. Sometimes I need only hear the tone of voice to know if they can use my true service, my mission of hope. I can tell almost as soon as I pick up the phone.

Take the one yesterday. Right away, I felt her attic could contain no fit target for one of the last dimly glowing corpses beneath the head-high elephant grass.

"I see in da papah heah dat ya clean out attics?" she said.

I wore a tie, and I scraped together enough coins atop the dresser of my flophouse room to take the D train. She sat on her stoop's bottom step. One eye beneath her puffball beret stayed fixed on me like the crosshairs of a sniper's rifle.

"Mrs. Rosenbaum?" I said.

Clearly she didn't associate my missionary-like attire with the attic cleaner she expected.

"Who told ya Mrs. Rosenbaum lived heah?" she said.

"You live here, don't you? Is Mrs. Rosenbaum in?"

The eye began to swivel. "Sometimes I live heah," she said, in a curling little aria of caginess. "I'm not shoah whether Mrs. Rosenbaum is in. Maybe if ya'd state ya business, I could find out for ya."

"It's about a portrait," I said. "But perhaps I have the wrong party."

"A porch-reht?" The eye whirled like an antenna gone haywire. "I don't know anything about any porch-reht. Whadid ya say ya name was?"

"But does Mrs. Rosenbaum know about a portrait? Or perhaps a bundle of letters? One that she might have misplaced?"

"No, I'm very shoah Mrs. Rosenbaum hasn't said anything about any porch-reht or any lettahs. I'm shoah you can't have any business like that heah."

So I knew it was just that, between scurrying off to going-out-of-business sales and evicting tenants whose infants' crying gave away the secret they existed, there wasn't time to clean the attic herself.

As I turned to go, the eye locked on target.

"Ya just ahtah know I'm gahnah remembah ya face."

"Perhaps Mrs. Rosenbaum will also remember it," I said.

"I'm very shoah that Mrs. Rosenbaum is gahnah remembah it."

Now you have marked me down as a cheap ethnic humorist and bigot, when I am nothing of the kind. In fact, my stint as a cleaner of attics has stripped away even those subliminal bigotries that make a normal life possible. A life, that is, spent on ground and second floors, choosing to eat and beget and study accounting and observe the seasons with pumpkins and painted eggs, rather than bump the spine against rafters and rummage through the detritus left by the grinding edge of lives led below hatches.

Or perhaps you write me off as a cracked philosopher. Granted, I believe attics to be the spiritual catacombs of humanity. Interred there, in trunks crammed with letters and photographs and certificates verifying birth, death and years of service, and among outmoded suits and shoes and skis and lawn chairs, perhaps used once and then hidden forever away, are the remains of life's most precious and painful moments, remains that evoke those moments' promise and unfathomable loss. Even inferior attics often yield up artifacts worthier of a philosopher's contemplation than any cuneiform tablet or Yorick's skull.

Yet I disclaim the title of philosopher, having for the sake of my ministry long since forgone the philosophical remove. I deny too that I am cracked. The one abnormality that I confess is a faculty grown overdeveloped through searing circumstance, like the arm strength of an amputee whose missing arm was severed by machine gun fire.

"Ah, an obfuscator and cheap jolter of sensibilities!" you exclaim. "Now we have his number." You mistake the exercise of my faculty for willfulness. It is as normal a human faculty as eating or begetting or winding clocks or entering numbers in ledgers. It has become the sole principle of my existence. In you, it is residual, nearly extinct, like the whale's leg. You live only at the grinding edge of life. I live only far behind it. It is my mission to project before your eyes emanations from the vast reaches behind that edge, emanations that may shock or disgust you, but that may also prove your salvation.

For example: Suppose I should produce a painting of a lovely Circassian girl shrinking from a turbaned, bejowled customer in an Ottoman brothel, and tell you that it is your sister. Your sister, let us suppose further, having been abandoned by one husband, is now unhappily married to another, and she is at this moment, with the faint lisp she never lost, speaking on the culture of geraniums to her garden club in Ohio.

"An outrage!" you bluster, when I offer as representing your sister an image very different from a wan, pinched face with lips lisping "straw mulch" above a midwestern podium. Yet which of us is more false to that creature of baffling tears and chameleon beauty, who from earliest childhood you knew to be doomed to some nameless injustice, and who is still, and will ever be, your sister? See what your pertinacity costs you!

~ * ~

Do not feel dismayed if at first you cannot see them. That will come in time.

There are only twelve of them, yet somehow they fill the valley. From the thin, sinuous line of green, head-high grass amid an expanse of grass that's instead brown and dry, you know a stream seeps the valley's length. Although it is a very narrow valley, the running men, their helmets and flak jackets flashing briefly into view, appeared to take up little of it. Fallen, they quite fill it. They died running, without a sound, and they fell without sound.

I will tell you a little of what they were like. One was a boy upon the backs of whose hands the tendons worked like accordion folds when he crumpled ration cans. One was Black, and from his nose you thought the cigarette smoke would never stop streaming. One would cry out balefully and lurch upright, swinging one arm, if you walked near him while he slept. One, when on patrol, would cradle his rifle in his arms and whisper to it tenderly, even as the razorlike edges of elephant grass lacerated the backs of his hands. One would squat, an elbow on knee, with his forearm and hand, palm-up, relaxed forward with the grace of a speaker exhorting his audience. One had a squarish Celtic head. One had a smooth face with sweat stains like tear streaks. One liked to talk, was wounded, and came back silent.

That was before the bullets' impact jarred the leaves on their helmets' netting and they died running and fell instantly, as killed soldiers fall.

The leaves on my helmet, too, quivered. I too fell faster than you could well believe. But, unlike the falling of the others, mine made a slight sound.

~ * ~

I was told the photograph had been found tucked beneath the stretcher strap over my chest. A combat photographer with the corpsmen must have put it there. For lost and wretched months spent in VA rehab, in YMCAs and in cheap boarding houses, I wished he had written something—geographic coordinates, his own unit, even just his name—on the back of it. I found it on the gleaming steel table beside my hospital bed. I propped it against the plastic water carafe before the night nurse came through the ward to drop the rattan blinds over the broad, screened windows.

By next evening, I could see them.

An ambulatory patient on orderly duty picked up the photograph when he sprayed the table with disinfectant. "This anything special to you?" he asked, holding it by a corner and flapping it.

"It's dead Marines," I told him.

He squinted at it. "It's nothing but elephant grass," he said. "A strip of green grass, then brown grass stretching away beyond it."

I felt too weak to try to show him. "Put it back on the table," I said. After the night nurse tried to take it away, I kept it under my pillow.

When I could leave the ward, I drew up a list with the unit name and the names of the men who had fallen and, as best I could remember, the places they came from. Then I asked to see the hospital commander.

In the heat outside the ward building, along walkways between glaring white dunes, bandaged and limping men crept like bacteria beneath a sterilizing lamp.

When the commander leaned back from his desk, the white bar of the fluorescent ceiling light hung suspended in the tinted lenses of his aviator sunglasses.

"For your own good, your own peace of mind, I urge you to drop the idea," he said.

"It doesn't seem much to ask," I told him.

"On the contrary. It is simply everything."

"Just their addresses? Or their next-of-kins'?"

He leaned motionless in his swivel chair. The bar of glare across his eyes seemed a sterile inversion of the black bar in police magazine photographs. Then, keeping his eyes lowered, he tilted forward and took my file from his desk. When he leaned back, folding open the swamp-green cover of the folder, the white bar dropped into place across his eyes.

"My dear fellow," he said, "as far as we and any others from whom you might seek information are concerned, you never belonged to the unit you name. Your unit was—" And he read the unit name that was on all my orders, a name that had nothing to do with the dozen men who fell silently. I had long assumed the unit name on my orders was there solely for arcane administrative reasons.

"But the others," I said, reaching for the photograph in the shirt pocket of my hospital pajamas, but then stopping short, having sensed something that had to do with the aseptic, glaring sand, the sterile bar across the eyes, the throb of the freeze machine in the hospital's distant morgue.

"No members of your unit were found with you," the commander said. "Officially, you were found alone."

~ * ~

Perhaps you can easily envision my futile sallies against the dense and, as it seemed, malevolently compounded obscurity. I will not bore you with a catalogue of my letters to congressmen. All made the same inquiry: whether the body of a certain Marine had been recovered, and if not, whether a certain sector had been closely searched. All the letters were referred to the Pentagon, whence they returned bearing a rubber-stamped inscription that must have wrung, with its faceless sneer, hearts more aching and anxious than mine: "Without service number and unit name, query lacks processable content." When my later letters returned, they bore an additional stamp. Despite its vaguely threatening message—"Correspondent is advised to adjust or cease mode of inquiry"—it inspired me briefly with hope.

As I tore open one after another of the letters that bore the double stamp, I noticed the two inscriptions always overlapped. That was notable because unnecessary, since ample white space remained below my succinct query. Comparing the letters, I saw it was always the same two corners that overlapped. As I spread the letters out on a desk in the VA dormitory room where I spent my final weeks of rehab, the man himself, the clerk, seemed to materialize. I glimpsed the unvarying tilt of the hat upon the dapper, graying head as morning by morning he entered his cubicle. I saw the deft incision with the letter knife, the caffeine-induced tremor of his hands un-stapling the congressional letterhead from the query beneath, the moment of recognition, the brisk irritation—a pinch of the lips, a single shake of the head—as eyes with a slight thyroidal bulge skipped from salutation to signature. I saw his forefinger, arched like that of the Sistine Jehovah, spin a Lazy Susan device filled with rubber stamps. I saw his hands pluck two worn handles from their clips, saw the piston-swift alternation of the descent upon the ink pad and then, with his immaculate elbows almost jauntily akimbo, their descent upon the letter.

But the hope died swiftly there beneath the rusted gooseneck lamp on the letter-strewn desk in the shabby VA dorm. I choked off the impulse to write one letter more, to reach my large, wasted but diurnally strengthening hand toward the small, deft, trembling hand, with the salutation, "O knight of the overlapping standard!"

Why did I fail to reach out? Because I had not yet learned to trust, beyond all palpability, the fellow man whose reality sprang from spiritual suffering and need. It was because, in short, I still shared your grinding-edge normalcy.

But my tutelage had hardly yet begun.

~ * ~

How to make you see the tawny evening sunlight sifting through soiled blinds and curtains and pooling upon the frayed carpets in the dozen seedy rooms in the dozen cities and towns and lost hamlets? From those windows, I looked out upon the greening copper dome of a Southern courthouse, upon the dolorous Dantean moil of Flatbush Avenue, upon the clean, Doric thrust of grain elevators against the sky. In the wane of afternoons when the rattle of pneumatic hammers and the rumble of warehouse doors and the drifting voices, even the whish of automobile tires, took on the spent, peaceful quality of hearts wending supper-ward, I would doubtingly hold up the photograph among the amber tresses of that light. I would once more count the dozen bodies, edged with a faint phosphorescence, strewn along the ribbon of tropic green. Doubtingly I held it, because during the days, until that evening light evoked them, I wondered in anguish whether they were truly there.

Mornings, I pored over telephone books and city directories. My separation pay and disability payments dribbled away in phone fees and bus fares. Fully half the time, a call did not suffice. To my question whether a son or nephew had been reported missing in a certain month and in a certain sector, the voice on the line would ask angrily what business it was of mine. Or, though answering in the negative, the voice would turn choked and hesitant. And there were the households without phones. When I had entered on my list as many addresses as I could hope to check before my scarred bowels would start to convulse with fatigue, I would ask the room clerk how to reach the first address, and tell him I would stay another night.

And then the bus ride to tenement or suburb, or the costly trip by taxi to a spruce but modest retirement bungalow or a ramshackle farm. You will understand how essential these visits were when I tell you the sight of my wounds nearly always dispelled mistrust and fear. Once seen, I could depend on solicitous honesty from the man or woman who had cursed me for a fraud over the telephone. So perhaps I can be forgiven for having remained so long fixated on the testimony of the flesh, and blind to what that light with tawny and maternal tenderness was trying to tell me.

There came moments in a few of those homes when I was certain I'd found what I sought. As I spoke of one among the twelve who had fallen soundlessly, hands would fly to parted lips, eyes would swooningly close or would widen as though with horrified recognition. At length, attic hatches would swing open, ladders on telescoping frames would slide down with their rusted springs lodging arthritic protest. The draped portraits that were too wrenchingly painful to be hung below hatches (only long after the time I speak of did I come to think of first and second floors as below hatches) would be fetched down and, with trembling hands, hovered over by my no less trembling heart, unswathed.

And, strange to say, I cannot tell you whether any of the faces in those photographs were the fleshly ones I believed it my duty to seek. Two framed portraits I borrowed, hoping that examination by the light of evening would resolve the matter. Such was the trust I inspired that the gaunt wife of an Alabama foundryman handed over without a word a portrait of—I was half convinced, though the unit, the month and year and the sector cited on MIA papers that the sulfurous Birmingham atmosphere had tinged with brown, all were wrong—one who had squatted with elbow on knee and forearm extended with hortatory grace. A Black machinist in oil-drenched coveralls glanced at a woman twice his size who wore the spotless uniform of a practical nurse before handing me the framed portrait of, I yearned to believe, him from whose nose smoke wispingly curled, as vapor curls from the nostrils of a bull in a frozen pasture.

You will, perhaps, have guessed the upshot of my breathless scrutiny, by evening light slanting through dust-laden blinds, of those retouched portrait photographs. Rather than vanishing, my hopes and my doubts expanded into a confusion that bloomed with the phosphorescent blooming of the corpses strewn within a pool of stagnant green, and that buzzed with the drowsy hum of the light itself—a humming that seemed to promise bliss instead of torment if I could attune myself to its frequency. I seemed to see in each of those portraits, burnished by that ocherous light, not any one of the dead men, but all of them. All of them, by that light's regressive logic, because the youth in each portrait was none of them.

Yet still my blindness persisted. I pursued my quest until I had exhausted the last phone directory in the last on my list of towns and crossroad post offices. I came upon several portraits more that I could not rule out. After my fruitless experience with the two borrowed portraits, however, I did not again ask to take one for closer scrutiny.

And when on the last evening of all I returned to the final YMCA corridor and unlocked the door to the final seedy room, I knew with a searing stitch in my wounded guts that the end was come, and that it was bitter. I dragged a rickety chair to an exhaust-smudged window, hoping that the waning sunlight, filled with golden motes dancing like souls in ether divine, might caress and restore me, as it had done in so many other wretched rooms. Instead, she had abandoned me. My lovely, maternal light had swept back into some empyreal sphere and left me sick, beaten, and alone.

For how many days and nights I sat motionless at that window, waiting for the light to return, I do not know. I recall going once to the door and opening it. There were a voice and a face, though I don't remember what the face looked like or what the voice said. To them I paid money, doubtless for the room.

Of the days and nights before and after that journey to the door, I recall little except that my will and vital functions seemed suspended. Only at great intervals did I thirst, and I never hungered. On frigid nights, the room's radiator stayed cold as a stone, yet I remained, short-sleeved, in my chair at the window.

I awoke from my stupor on a night cold enough for me to see my breath, even in the darkness. Lifting the blinds and blinking upward, I thought I saw my beloved light hovering behind the Pleiades. And I thought that amid its veiling tresses, it grieved—not for my private defeat and suffering, but for its failure to teach one upon the earth to be its emissary.

I kept my vigil until dawn erased the Pleiades. Then I tottered to my closet and packed my duffel.

~ * ~

My quest over for flesh from whom sprang twelve men who had fallen soundlessly within a ribbon of head-high grass, I stumbled on across the continent, groping now simply for that sweet light. I sought it in sunsets above mesas seen through the tinted windows of buses, and in the cat's-eye flicker of revolving ornaments above beer taps. After weeks of unloading huge furnace bricks and scurrying along catwalks with troughs of gooey mortar balanced on my shoulder, I desperately and foolishly sought that tender light in the firing of an enormous kiln. I sought it in brothels, in tent meetings and at celebrations of Catholic and High Anglican Mass. And in all the turned-aside, brittlely indifferent cheeks of the whores, in the sawdust haze about arms that jerked in frenzied exhortation inside the tents, in the flicker of tapers and sheen of surplices above altar rails, I found that dear light not.

It returned, as perhaps it must, when no longer hoped for or sought. Often in those days when I would turn from liquor and prostitutes to weeks of brutal labor to trance-like attendance in the ragged tents of bush league evangelists, I would suddenly and in panic flee a city and the avatar of my obsession that I had there pursued. Oh, you who think I had departed from your grinding-edge precepts: no such thing! When the revulsion struck, I would dash for the exit like the uninsured father of six at a cry of fire, and with the same sense of danger avoided and duty flown to. On this occasion, I scrambled aboard the milk-run bus for the city where, without clear purpose or hope, I had decided to alight next.

As I swung my duffel onto the rack above the first row of seats on the driver's side, a baggage clerk appeared on the lower step. He held a small, square, sturdy-looking cardboard box on his lifted palm. "Human remains," he said in a nasal blat.

The driver, a graying specimen of droop-featured and large-eared benignity, who stood by the steering wheel wetting his thumb and leafing through tickets, stared at the box. "Human what?" he said.

"Remains, ashes," the young clerk blatted. "There'll be a woman to pick them up at Medina Store."

With the hand holding the sheaf of tickets, the driver made a truncated motion toward his hat, as though he would remove it in respect. "What am I supposed to do with them?" he said.

"Take 'em to her," the clerk said. He balanced the box on his fingertips and gazed at it with his head cocked. "Understand he died of a heart attack in bed last night. Funeral home fetched the body down here this morning for cremation. Widow figured bus would be cheaper for the return trip. Didn't want it to go baggage, though. Wants the driver to carry it."

The driver put the tickets and his punch on his seat and cleared his throat. He took the box gingerly, with both hands. He looked at the two empty front seats across the aisle from me and placed the box in the window seat. He stood for a few moments looking askance at the box, then turned and rummaged in a compartment in his dashboard. He took out a magazine and placed it in the aisle seat next to the box.

The baggage clerk smirked. "Figure he'll want to read?" he said.

The driver frowned, and his earlobes reddened. "I was marking the seat," he said. "Seems right to keep that seat empty, don't you think?"

"Do-hon't ask me," the clerk said, stepping down backward from the bottom step and raising both hands, palms forward. "You're the professor."

Can you, smug and replete by your fireside or your easy chair lamp, imagine the joy that tremblingly unfurled and fluttered aloft in my breast when, as the bus pulled from the station, a shaft of tawny light, humming like a distant swarm of bees on a windless August afternoon, stole across the box and the cover of that news magazine? Can you picture the effect of that light upon the white dust—pulverized concrete—that coated the helmet and forearms of a man whose seamed face was the hue and texture of crumbling pavement on peaceful rural roads?

He flagged the bus beside a girder-strewn wasteland, and he greeted the driver by name. As the driver prepared a ticket, the big construction worker scanned the seats crowded with commuting laborers and domestics. His eyes, bloodshot at the corners, came to rest sidelong on the box in the front window seat. As he read the box's label, he smiled tenderly.

When the driver handed him the ticket, the big man picked up the magazine and eased into the aisle seat beside the box. With an envious gasp, I saw the light clasp like a welcoming bride his helmet and face and bare forearms. Like a grateful, familiar beloved, he shut his eyes and let his head loll back, and that sweet light he seemed to breathe in.

"I'll keep the gen'leman company," he said. The driver scowled and briefly fidgeted, but said nothing.

When the bus was underway again, my thirst-crazed soul could no longer forgo a draught of the nectar it craved. I slid into the aisle seat and stretched forth my hand. My fingers reached the light. O, bliss un-nameable! My eyes closed in tearful rapture. The bus jolted, and my palm smacked a massive forearm.

The pink-edged eyes in a face that seemed arrested in an advanced state of peaceful crumbling were already upon me, without resentment or surprise, when my eyes opened. We both blinked in the dust rising from his forearm.

"It's powerful soothing, ain't it, son?" he said.

"Yes," I said. Confusion and defensiveness overrode my joy. "The light, you mean. You know it too."

"*Know* it?" he laughed. "*Know* that light? Son, ain't I lived fifty-eight years with it? Ain't I studied it till I can slip into it most every evening 'bout this time? Ain't I found out there ain't much else *worth* studying?"

"Then maybe you..." It seemed too much to hope. Never yet, since I had shown it to the hospital commander, had I shown the photograph to anyone. It was in my shirt pocket now, as always. "Maybe you can help me," I said. "Maybe you can tell me if I really see something, or if I only think that I..." I drew forth the photograph, still hesitant. But when I saw his broad, steady, split-nailed fingers uplifted in that light, my hand with the photograph moved swiftly toward them.

"Look, you don't even need to tell me what they are," I babbled. "Just if there's anything there at all. If you can see something glowing. It always used to be this time of day, in this light, that I could see them. I thought, since you said you—"

"It's dead boys," he said softly, though still with an undertone of gentle laughter. He balanced the photograph on his fingertips, above the soiled palm. He did not even squint, as I had always needed to do. "It's a whole valley full of dead boys, son. That's what you seen." He handed back the picture. In the fine Vesuvian ash upon his forearm, I saw an ancient palm print: my own.

"Then maybe you could even..." I felt it was impossible, but already I had been granted more than I could have dreamed. I grasped the forearm, felt a dry slipperiness as if the concrete dust were graphite. "I know it's ridiculous to even ask," I said. "But if you could try to tell me ... who they are?"

This time his laughter seemed tinged by the grief I had seen in the light in its retreat beyond the Pleiades.

"Why son, no wonder you're so peaked-looking, if that's what's been fretting you. Why, look here, son," he said softly, opening one hand toward the box on the seat beside him. "They're him."

My claim may border on sacrilege, yet it's true: My enlightenment was as sudden as Paul's on the road to Tarsus. I at last saw that my quest had not failed. I saw that each of the men whose next-of-kin I had sought, and no less the man who had died mere hours before, lay now, and would lie forever, in that valley of dead Marines.

But there was something more.

"You're making progress already, son." I must have frowned uncomprehendingly. He laid a forefinger on the photograph. "See, you've done got rid of one of them now."

With my own trembling forefinger, I counted the humped, glowing corpses. There were only eleven.

~ * ~

And so, made whole myself, to make you whole I came up here, among the moose heads and parcheesi sets, the ancient phonographs and occasional snakeskins. I'm certainly not up here for fun. Don't think for a moment that I wouldn't rather be down below at your steaming breakfast table, smiling with you at your little ones when they shiver at the snarling that you recognize as the sound of the weighty headboard of your late parents' mahogany bedstead being dragged across attic boards. Ah, but your little ones are wiser than you! Wrestling with headboards and cedar chests, or breaching barricades of lawn furniture and croquet sets and boxed toys to lift dusty bedspreads from framed portraits, I do battle with monsters more terrible than any St. George's dragon. Rarely can I slay them. It lies within neither my purpose nor my power to turn them into house pets. But, by hooking my fingers in their nostrils and pounding home a dead Marine, or summoning you up when a certain light prevails, I can perhaps inoculate you against the fiery breath that, next morning or on the day twenty years hence when you tear open a telegram envelope, will roar down through your ceiling and reduce to cinders your waffles and newspaper and fresh tablecloth.

"You really expect us to accept this tangled tale in lieu of seminary parchment, ordination, testimonials of demons cast out in Botswana?" you snort. Sheathe your bright scorn, for despite the minimal humidity in your attic, grinding-edge passions rust quickly up here. You may fare very well below hatches with that bridle of the head and curl of the lip. But, stooping as you must when a rafter impends above your neckbone, that scornful grimace merely makes you look ridiculous. If you will not accept my true service, then leave me to my labor. Rest assured your rejection will not inflate my modest fee.

"Impertinent, impious charlatan!" you mutter as you descend. "Takes our short-windedness in these stifling quarters for breathless heed. Then, when we dare contradict his ravings, he boots us out of our own attics. Some missionary!"

True, I no longer trifle with those who will not acknowledge a need. As the end draws near, my patience shortens. I dread as I do death the day when my charge will be lifted, when the last flak-jacketed corpse within the elephant grass will vanish. Yet would I hurry that final day on. I yearn for its absolving balm, as I yearn also for death.

Already more than half of them are gone. Do not debase yourself with your grinding-edge lust for precision.

My chief regret is that my successes have been so nearly exclusively with women. Not that those victories were any the less sweet in themselves. Take the widow in Sandusky who scrambled eggs for me below hatches, while up above I wrestled, not with the ghost of the husband she revered, but with that of the long-distance truck driver with whom she had conceived her first child. Or the travel writer who, doubtless with nostrils flaring like those of the Arabian stallion she loved to ride along Sheepshead Bay, had attacked with her fists an astonished Afghan, who pinched her in the market of a lawless town where novel firearms were manufactured, and who she knew to be armed with the pistols in the form of fountain pens he hawked.

That razor-edged Manhattanite sought to pull her trembling hand from my firm one as I led her toward the spot beneath an attic skylight where I had positioned a wicker armchair. In that chair (please credit me with the clairvoyance my faculty has spawned), her daughter had loved to sit with one foot curled beneath her as she read. The foot inevitably went to sleep, and the mother as inevitably gave one of the brusque, lightsome scoldings that were her sole expression of tenderness.

The daughter had died, absurdly, of blood poisoning contracted through a cat scratch. Her mother, in her irritation at an airline agent's bungling, had ridiculed her daughter for fretting about the scratch. In that chair the girl, mortified, her head bowed, had burrowed the scratched hand beneath a leg of her jeans, while the mother recounted the scratches and sprains she herself had gamely ignored on five continents.

She would rather have braved Khyber-fuls of lecherous tribesmen armed to their goatlike ears with loaded fountain pens and walking sticks, than have faced that chair in the ocherous evening sunlight that now bathed it. I willed my strength into her writhing frame, while with my free hand I held the photograph like a compass up to the light until the glow of one of the bodies dissolved and I felt the mortal battle within that proud creature—on her knees now, and with her arms outstretched upon the arms of the chair—give way to gasping, grateful sobs.

There can be no regretting victories such as these. Still, would that there had been more men than that Tennessee county attorney. In his parlor, the two of us sipped muscadine wine from sherry glasses, and crimped the lees between our teeth. Then, taking up shears and straw hat and tucking a bandanna beneath the back of the brim so that, legionnaire-wise, it shielded his florid bull neck, he shambled toward his arbor. I, donning spiritual pea jacket and sou'wester, mounted to the attic.

Topside, I cleared away and belayed down, swaying easily on my sea legs (the sole nautical attribute most Marines acquire) while that white clapboard schooner of a farmhouse, her porch balustrade bared in a shark-like grimace, champed a bone of well-tended japonicas in bloom. Presently, as evening sunlight began to filter through louvers, a chill, buffeting wind set in from a quarter where I had noticed a small, strap-bound trunk.

Opening the lid of this Aeolian trunk, I found the gusts issued from beneath the flap of an unmarked and unsealed envelope. I extracted a newspaper clipping. "NY Times" and a date two years prior were scribbled along one edge. It announced the engagement of a Columbia student—the county attorney's son—and a ballerina with a prominent New York company. There was no photograph of the couple.

Bereft! Bereft, I say, of the power to turn aside! For what comparative bliss it would have been to re-fold that clipping and return it to its envelope with a smile or a sigh. I do not speak of the arctic blast from off the creased newsprint. For that I had merely to tug down my spiritual sou'wester and wrap the floppy collar of my pea jacket into a stout blue cone about my ears. But what defense had I against the true terrors of those polar time-seas, against the tide that now rolled down upon me with your monster riding gape-jawed on its crest?

"Whence these mythic dragons, this bugbear horror?" you scoff. But acerbity drains from your voice, your eyebrows half-credulously lift. You discover that you really hope to find something more than a looney batting away at stuffed, shooting-gallery Nessies, especially when he seems to claim something grandiose about your own inner reaches.

Store your garden shears in your back pocket and descend your stepladder to the shadow-stippled floor of the cool, rustling corridor of trellised vines. Yank the bandanna from the back of your hat and, mopping your face, shamble with a gouty hitch toward your porch. Globs of evening sunlight will roll like anointing myrrh down your stooped shoulders, but you need pay the light no heed just yet. Hearken not, as you toss your straw hat upon a hall-tree horn, for scuffling and thrashing above. Struggles as titanic as mine with your monster play out in utmost silence. See: Through a hall window whose blind your wife yanked up to glance out at you before fastening a recalcitrant earring and hurrying off to her weekly bridge party—see the evening sunlight fall upon the attic ladder, enveloping each metal rung in a soft semblance of St. Elmo's fire. If it clears your pipes and makes you feel less awkward, harrumph as you ascend the ladder, and avow you don't see how flesh and blood can withstand a half day's labor in a ninety-degree attic with no liquid fortification but a glass of muscadine wine.

Permit me to introduce you. This fellow, whose head I hold swiveled with his neck clamped within my elbow, and whose crimson nostrils flutter in a way that leads you to expect a labored rattling instead of this utter silence, was born right here, topside. It was on a morning of that summer when you took the profound adolescent plunge into idleness. It was the kind of summer morning when space and time seem dissolved into an oppressive stickiness that pins you to your sweat-soaked mattress, and you cannot distinguish the flat clank of the bell of a cow being let out to pasture a mile away and three hours ago from the bell your mother now angrily rings at the foot of the stairs to roust you out of bed.

Your mother ordered you to clean the attic with a hired Black girl whom you had never seen before. At first you chewed the aloof cud of affronted manhood. But when there had diffused upon the stifling attic air the aroma of wilted orchids, and you realized it was the odor of the girl's sweat, something happened in your stomach that felt like the winking on of a lightning bug's light.

What you felt in your stomach was this fellow's birth. You will remember that when your mother called you down for lunch, she took one look at your face and a longer look at the girl's face with its downcast eyes and crescent eyelids and the smooth, taut sweep from her cheekbone to her delicate chin. When lunch was over, your mother looked at you again, and then she wasn't looking at you, but was pushing back a lock of her hair and, in a voice that like her eyes seemed directed just above and beyond your shoulder, was saying Frances should be able to finish the attic by herself, and if you wished you could take the car and go to the grocery and buy some cigarettes. And you knew that the reason she spoke toward the point beyond your shoulder was that if she spoke to your face, you could not help mentioning that there was a carton of cigarettes in the bag of groceries you carried in from the car for her yesterday. You will recall that, as you settled behind the steering wheel, thinking of your mother's eyes and of the dark sheen beneath the girl's cheekbone and the scent of orchids in a state of incipient decay, you felt the smooth, wobbling lizardhead slide out onto your diaphragm.

"But that was just a newt, not this Komodo dragon!" you cry. Hugest reptiles from tiniest wrigglers grow, my friend. I assure you this grisly, foam-flecked muzzle is what then lay tinglingly on your diaphragm like a drop of golden liqueur.

Now a look of rapturous relief overspreads your face. "The jewel!" you exclaim, pointing at the top of the pinioned head. "It has no jewel!"

But don't you remember? Your own hand plucked the jewel from the head of the rosy, transparent-skinned little salamander that you had come to regard as a benign familiar. It was on an April night during your own stint in the city. You waited until the law library closed and then hurried alone through the west eighties. By the time you came in sight of the street corner where the week before you had heard, out of the fog, the soft Negroid accents that in memory belonged with fine, slanting cheekbones and an odor of crushed orchids, the lizard had its head and shoulders wedged into your gullet and was tearing at your stomach with its hind claws, struggling to get out.

Please, spare us both your mortified blushes. In the cotton-batting atmosphere up here and your already overheated state, they can do you no good. The tale of your role in his escape is safe with me. I regard attic boards awash in the light you see about us as a priest does a confessional.

It was your plucking of the jewel that gave this big boy his freedom and his growth, that ridge of barbed spines and those saw-edged, perfectly occluding jaws. Oh, he's yours, all right. Just step closer and see the scarred depression, the jewel's socket, in his head. You were not quite wrong in believing you got rid of him in that malodorous hotel that foggy night. But the trouble with giving these rascals their freedom is that they cease to be familiars without ever really departing the premises. They may lurk, quiescent, for decades in odd corners of lee decks, and then take a sudden notion to lope about among the crew, snapping off arms and legs. You can tell from the caked blood and bits of shriveled flesh at the corners of this fellow's jaws that he has had his battening spree. Shall I remind you whose blood and flesh? That of your son, and of the Black ballerina and grandson whom you have vowed never to see. And your wife's. And, of course, your own.

And now, skepticism to the winds, uttering a mooselike sob of despair, you advance with lifted shears aimed at the spot where the creature's noisome, milky under-flesh throbs. That's the spirit! But not yet the way. Your role awaits you below. Its instrument is the telephone, and it will imbrue you not in spouting reptile blood but, most likely, in unmanly tears. So best not wait for your wife's return.

Besides, this baby, who has again started lashing his tail and twisting his jaws in my grip, is exclusively your own monster. Your wife can't help us quench his spirit of fun. There might be one of her own hibernating over there behind that rack of dresses in zippered, clear plastic bags with mothballs in their bottoms. But at present we must deal solely with Sweetness here.

Quickly now, while the evening light still filters through the louvers. My part in this business is certain to be long-drawn and messy. Frankly, I don't want you about, retching and swooning while you yet gaze horror-struck as I hammer a dimly glowing dead Marine through its heart.

And be sure to close the hatch behind you. Once Daisy Breath here perceives my mortal intent, the frolic will truly start. Should he then twist from my grasp and escape down the hatch, he will in ultimate panic, in fetal reversion, try to leap down your throat. Then there'll be hell to pay.

In lubberly agitation you move toward the hatch. At its verge you pause and frown. Gouts of sweat drip from your face and, in the midwatch silence, burst like grenades upon the deck.

"But if the rosy newt inside my gut can have grown so huge and hideous, then what doubly loathsome creature must my son have spawned?" you breathe in cloddish stage soliloquy.

Hence! Before driven out of all patience I release upon you your true progeny! How dare you presume that the man who by grinding-edge convention you call your son shares your propensity for the spontaneous generation of newts? In your son's case, love is by far the more probable answer. Dress that maxim in jungle fatigues and flak jacket and dip it in firefly phosphorescence, and you have the bodkin that will give Sugar-Bunch his quietus: Love is forever the more probable answer.

Suppose a tiny doglike snout did nuzzle at your son's diaphragm the night he first watched her glide and pirouette and bend like a dew-weighted flower on the spotlit stage. Certainly, he did not pluck the jewel from his salamander's head, as you had done. And so it remained a small, bright, smooth, transparent-skinned familiar lying curled in his stomach. At night, in bed beside her, he must feel its jewel glowing, and in his mind see the jewel's soft fire reflected within the creature's mild lidless eyes, all pupil, in the darkness of his vitals.

Hence, I say! Ah, you are gone already, and my histrionic sally has been played to an audience of one large lizard. The hatch is shut, I see. I hear the whirr of a telephone dial below. Well, I'd best be about my end of the bargain.

Allow me to divert myself, as I perform that unpleasantness, by telling you about the madwoman in Brighton. Of course, you neither permit nor refuse, since you are down below, choking out the words that will shortly, in an unkempt apartment lined with law textbooks and baby photographs, unite you with three who—as you now put it, and in this case I applaud your grinding-edge presumption—belong to you. Still, you do me a great favor by letting me imagine you here, and letting me suppose that when I beg to tell you of the madwoman in Brighton, your ready nod stops short, as though you were already rapt. Regard my tale, if you choose, as the sort of fable hardened Marines tell, one that repackages in tolerable form truths learned in ghastly combat.

I was hunting for a Sunday *Times* on a chill October evening. I was having no luck, since it was Tuesday and the candy stores, which is where you buy newspapers in Brooklyn, had returned their Sunday issues. As I turned a corner, she raved at me from the entryway to a bakery.

"The gyps, the bastahds! I was a quatah shawat and they wouldn't give me credit for a quatah, o-ooh! I was hungry, I was stahvin, I didn't have nuttin in the place, and they wouldn't give me credit! Aftah all the business I done with the bastahds!"

Softly, with what seemed virtuosity, like a tympanist playing a complex, muted passage, she beat her fists upon the door, the baker's bay window and a tile wall. Below the rim of her black felt hat, topaz eyes streamed with grief. On a step of the doorway were two bags. A loaf of bread protruded from one of them. Blood seeped through the paper of the other bag, which contained something massive and bulbous.

"They'll regret it the longest day they ever lived, the gyps!" she sobbed.

I laid a hand on her arm. Behind her distended, streaming face I saw a demon howling with glee at its sport.

"How much is it you need?" I said. The demon leered at me for a fool, but I knew my part and kept up my bluff.

"O-oh, I dahnt kno-ow," she bawled. "Maybe a dol-lah."

I pressed a bill into her palm. Behind me I heard a sandpapery chuckle.

"Ah, whadda mush-head," the rasping one said.

"I beg your pardon?" I said with cold dignity. As I turned, I felt the scratch of needle eyes that were too small and close together to rake rather than mildly prick.

"Sho-ah," Needle Eyes said, rolling aside an overlong torso that was humped like a weasel's. When he whipped the torso toward me, the eyes worked like a whip's snapper. "Shoah yah a mush-head. Rosie's just shopping. Thanks ta mush-heads like you, she'll go home with dose bags fulla crap, and worse dan crap."

"Explain yourself, sir," I demanded. I could feel the demon lying crouched and attentive behind the woman's raving.

"Whatsa mattah, ya deaf?" The eyes pronged at me like a Lilliputian pitchfork. "Dat's da way Rosie shops, I'm tellin' yah. She stands outside places and cries dat da people won't give her whateveh she wants 'cause she's a quatah shawat. Mosta da time de proprietor comes out and gives her whateveh it is she wants so she'll quit scarin' away business. But once in a while a mush-head comes along dat figyahs a quatah's worth of feelin' sorry for Rosie'll set him straight wid da world. But when ya mush-head stops and says somethin' mush-headed to Rosie, it turns out she's a dollah shawat. Now ya mush-head takes too much pride in bein' a mush-head to just turn and walk away, see?"

"I told 'em da rats got da bagels!" the woman raved. "They want me ta hock my rings so they can make a mint outa me, da robbahs!"

The drumming of a train on the elevated tracks above us briefly drowned out her lament.

"Yeah, shoah," Needle Eyes said, with that cynical wheeling aside and returning whip of the weasel torso. "Shoah yah old man's got rats in his place."

"But it's true she's hungry," I said, lamblike, lulling the demon.

"Listen," Needle Eyes said, suddenly confidential. He clutched the collar of my fatigue jacket. "Her old man's got plenty. He's a landlahd, see? He's got two houses over on Brighton Sixth. Rats, she tells yah? Listen. He's got so many poitahreecans shoehahned into dose places dat da rats ain't got a chance."

"Then why does she beg in the streets this way?" I said, still playing bumpkin in boxing gloves, waiting for the instant the smirking demon would drop its guard.

"Whaddaya mean *why*?" Needle Eyes spat out the offensive word as though it were a bitter pit. "Because she's nuts! Because her old man dahn't care what da hell she does! He's got an appliance stoah and two dumps wid poitahreecans hangin' out da windahs and fightin' each otheh for da privilege of campin' on da fiah escapes. He's got a whore down in Sea Gate dat HIAS brought oveh dat's learned just enough English ta get her hair dyed red. Ya can take one look at her and figyeh what a relief da Russians musta felt ta get dat much private enterprise outa da country on one ayahplane. So whaddas he care if Rosie gets da gahbidge she eats by cryin' in da street?

"*Why*, da guy asks me!" Needle Eyes informed circumambient sentience. "*Why*, ya wanta know? 'Cause if you wanta know *why*, misteh, den forget yah mush-headed kindsa whys. Go big-time wid yah whys, misteh. Figyah out why *dat*." And he pointed at the bulging bag, the bottom of which was now sodden with blood.

I flicked open my inward light meter. Not yet, but in another minute perhaps, the amber light I required for my work would spill down over the elevated tracks. I sauntered toward the bag. I opened it. I flinched not at the horrid breath it expelled. Behind me, Needle Eyes swapped the fine sandpaper of his earlier chuckle for a coarser grain.

"I told 'em da rats ate it up fastah dan I could get it inta da pantry," Rosie foamed, and she softly drubbed the door. "I told 'em I got a lock box on da stoop now to put it in. But da bastahds wouldn't belie-eeve me!"

The shop's balding proprietor appeared behind the glass panes in the door. As though the demon briefly bestrode him, his face contorted, and he made a savage gesture of eviction. Then he flipped the "Open" sign to "Closed" and yanked down the shade.

"A-aa-aaoh!" Rosie wailed, her head thrown back, the eyes beneath the black felt brim stark open and streaming.

I let the demon gloat over this turn of the screw while I awaited the light's tender cascade. I sensed the moment when the light swirled behind the near rail of the elevated track. I felt it tremble at the rail's verge.

Like the tresses of a Madonna leaning above me as I leaned to peer into the paper bag, the light spilled over my nape and curled about a chalky, scoured hog's head. I could tell from the sag of a shut eyelid that the eyes were out. The hog's feet, severed ends uppermost, were stuffed beside the head.

"Yeah, buddy," came Needle Eyes' rasping whisper. "Figyeh out why *dat*."

I drew erect. Like a decoy cop whipping out his badge to a confidence man, I whipped the worn, wrinkled photograph from my jacket pocket.

"O thou who were from all time anathema to a boy who swung one arm blindly if you walked near him while he slept," I intoned. "By his authority and armed with his power I command you: Leave this woman!"

At first, I suspected a misfire. Rosie stood stock still, not even blinking, though she drooled a little. I couldn't spot the demon, but that could simply mean it had scuttled out of range. Braced for a counterblow, I counted the dimly glowing corpses. One was gone, all right.

"I beg yah pardon, buddy," Needle Eyes rasped reverently. "I thought yah was just anotheh mush-head. I'd neveh have guessed yah was nuttiah yet dan Rosie."

I heard the smash and tinkle of breaking glass, and then a whoosh as of air rushing through a small opening. Then there was a scrambling sound inside the shop, and the proprietor began to yell in Yiddish.

I reached through the door's broken pane and pulled down on the blind to free its catch. When the blind shot up, I saw a big white and yellow cat springing across the floor with arched and bristling back. The aproned proprietor advanced behind the cat and swatted at the floor ahead of it with a broom. At first I thought he was trying to hit the cat and overshooting. But as they neared the door—the cat lashing out with its foreclaws and the man whamming in front of it—I saw that they both pursued a plump triangular shape that hopped crazily about like a jumping bean.

I jerked my face away from the door when I saw the shape take off, and as it flew out the broken pane, I caught a whiff of potato knish. Needle Eyes ducked the flying knish, and it bounded across the pavement and vanished down a curbside drain.

"Holy cheez!" Needle Eyes said. With his weasel hump and drained face, he resembled a flak-jacketed Marine sprinting through an ambush. "Do me a favah, misteh," he said. "Tell me I'm nuts, too. I think I prefeh dat interpretation."

"I told 'em I had ta move into da kitchen and let da rats take da rest!" Rosie burst out afresh. "I told 'em there ain't enough fiah in Brooklyn ta boin dose rats outa thah!"

"Tiss time you fine-tly done it, Rosie," the shopkeeper said behind the door. "Tiss time I fine-tly call da cops. I don't know vat da hell you trow in here und I don't vant to know. I let you tell da cops vat ta hell you trow."

In Rosie's face, I glimpsed the demon's leer. If it had kept Rosie quiet and stayed hidden, its ruse might have worked. But demons are stupid that way. Even when one has gotten a taste of your steel-jacketed specials, it can no more refrain from leering and tormenting its victim than a hunted hyena can lope past a dead zebra without taking a snack, or curb the bray that updates the veldt on its whereabouts.

The light was still with me. Again I held up the photograph.

"O, thou ancient and accursed!" I said. "By the grace of a Marine whose mighty lungs could draw up the flame-shot, sulfurous billows of thy proper abode and exude them sweetened and pure, I command thee! Depart this woman and this shore!" And I saw the largest of the glowing corpses grow dim, pulse like the expiring wick of a gasoline lantern, and vanish.

Far better is it to slay one of these babies rather than merely evict him, but also far more demanding on the sinew and spirit of the one who deals him his death. How the memory of that bounding knish lightens the grisly task, here in your stifling attic, of driving in the fatigue-clad spike, probing for the ventricle wall and waiting for the audible rip and the long shudder.

It wasn't that I'd missed Rosie's demon on my first try. It was just that demons are tough buggers, and when they get entrenched it's like trying to clear mealworms out of a potato cellar. I saw the demon wince as the second shot slammed home, but I also saw it scurry back into hiding, leaving Rosie's face frozen in a catatonic drool.

This time I was ready for the feint and kept my eyes on Rosie while the remaining door panes shattered and the flurry started again inside the shop. This time there must have been a dozen knishes. I could tell from the cat's receding screech that it had sized up the odds and headed for the back door. The shopkeeper must have been in back, on the phone to the police.

Before the knishes took flight, I wheeled another greenly glimmering cartridge up beneath the hammer of my mission and took aim at the wounded demon, cowering now behind that woman's heart like an oafish, comical bandit trying to take cover behind a rock half his size. And then I slowly squeezed off.

"O, thou who came from the void and must return to the void, and whose name is the void! By the grace of this Marine, who came from the void and whom I now return to the void, but whose name is all that is not the void, I command thee! Depart from this woman. Begone from the shores of humankind. Inhabit no more the bodies of men, nor those of creatures consecrate."

All might have gone well if I hadn't started to fancy the figure I was cutting and added that rhetorical fillip, "nor creatures consecrate." One of the things that can be taken to mean is something it's unwise to suggest to a demon in Brighton Beach, America's welcome mat for Russian Jews. Especially not when there's a pig's head and four serviceable feet inside a bag within easy vaulting distance.

As soon as I opened my mouth to utter a frantic addendum, I heard a rustling and clack of ankle bones from inside the bag. The snout ripped through the blood-soaked bag and the head shook its ears to free itself from the gummy paper. Hovering above the sidewalk, the head swerved like a compass needle while the feet scampered and swapped places beneath it like recruits falling in. When the feet were properly deployed, the head took a couple more practice turns and then zeroed its gape on me. It sprang and sank its teeth into the flesh above my knee. Down the street a woman screamed. From her distance, it must have looked like I was being attacked by a giant white rat on stilts.

Then it was that Needle Eyes showed his mettle. Or perhaps the mettle had been born in him as he watched me coolly fire off one dead Marine after another at the demon's stubborn leer. Rare is the soul that's too far gone in cynicism to be redeemed by the example of Marines hurtling bravely to their sacrificial destiny. So perhaps Needle Eyes' soul too was gathered in that day.

"Get ta hell inta da watah like he told yah, yah son of a bitch!" he yelled, and he cracked Rosie's loaf of bread, grown formidable with age, over the pig's pate.

Now I deserve your reproach. To buffer my own nerves from current trauma, I risk letting trail off into slapstick a story intended to give your sensibility, in parting, a salutary fine tuning. Worthy of its chronicler as is Needle Eyes' bold seizure of the head's ears and his stout grapple until its teeth ripped free of my pants leg, that chronicler must not be I. However that clattering chase along Brighton Beach Avenue and Brighton Second to the water's verge may beg for panoramic rendering (of aghast faces sweeping past, of shrieking and fainting women, of the fusillade of thrown-open windows resounding between cavernous tenement walls like firecrackers in a garbage can, of fruit rinds thrown from above in emulation of Needle Eyes' steady barrage of bread chunks and curses, and of the galloping and bucking head itself, astride which three helmeted, glimmering figures clung like broncobusters, with heels flying and arms thrown high)—however insistently that chase may plead for its historian, yet must I refrain, yet must I lash my yearning fast to the splintery, Ithacan mast of my mission.

For it is not sweep and scope that I must convey, not the flying tumult that ended as, limping and bleeding, I brought up the rear of the pursuit onto the sand between boardwalk pilings and saw that pig's head plow a zig-zag course through the surf, leaving a steaming wake, while Needle Eyes churned onward knee-deep in surf and hurled bread chunks, and from afar a police siren waxed shrill.

No. Rather, I must make you feel the emotion that rippled in my breast like a wind-whipped pennant as that gaping hog's head, bestrode by three plucky dead Marines the hue of fireflies' lamps, sank within a seething vortex in the shadow of a fishing pier.

Only one hallowed dispatch will serve to convey my emotion: The Marines had landed, and the beach was secure.

They had landed for the old mission, older by far than Tripoli or Iwo Jima. Though torment of the innocent be hidden on remotest shores, the Marines will be there. Toward wherever one soul is denied free passage or held for outrageous ransom, the Marines scud upon fawn-colored billows. O prison camp commandant lulled to thy noon nap by shrieks from thy fingernail extraction chambers—art thy dreams pricked by spume-flecked bayonets aslant and flashing above battleship rails? Gloatest thou, o sebaceous emir, over the heart that lies racked and groaning in thy Barbary dungeon? Hear, hear from afar the shout that goes up from the Marine-thronged decks of arrowing clippers! Pridest thyself, o Midwestern husband, o brother, on the forged links that bind a sibilant sprite to couch and garden club podium? What shall shield thee, o grinding edge potentate, when those chains dissolve into whining shrapnel under the massed fire of a leatherneck platoon, the lip of whose landing craft even now yawns forth and smites thy beach with a report like the crack of an empire's doom?

It's a bit out of fashion, I know, the feeling that unfurled in me as I limped from among wrack-festooned pilings toward the comrade who still crouched among light combers in a posture of furious onslaught, while between the cavern walls of Brighton Second an expiring siren moaned. It was pride that I felt on that hard-won beach. Pride that soared like the distant, fiery wheel above Coney Island, when behind the squad car windshield, I saw topaz eyes streaming. For the eyes beneath the brim of an amorphous felt hat streamed no more with crazed anguish, but with the gratitude and hope of a soul set free.

Yes pride, my friend. I felt proud to be a Marine.

But come. The beast is dead. For anxious moments I feared the spike would never reach its gristly, throbbing heart's wall. See: Only the leaves on a helmet's netting still show above the reptile breast, like feathers on a buried shaft. We can leave it to a certain mistress of mine to mop up this gore with her tawny hair.

Come. It is late, and I thirst. Help me secure the hatch—there. Our task is done. For tonight, let it bluster as it may topside. Let us suppose that Providence is pilot. Or let us suppose that it is not.

Fain would my spent heart fly to a dimpled glass decanter. Yes, my friend, I quite agree. We shall drink nothing but muscadine wine.

The Inland Sea

Marlise phoned yesterday to tell me about a package tour to India. She said we could get a Hindu wedding ceremony in Bombay for $180.

The wedding part was a joke. We're getting married in Highland Park. I don't know what her father will pay for it, but it won't be $180.

I'm afraid the rest of it wasn't a joke. It'll be still less of a joke when I tell her a Larchmont College English instructor's salary doesn't cover tours to India, and that I won't accept the trip as a gift from her father.

"Why India?" I asked her. "Does your dad's firm have business connections there?"

"Oh, no. I guess I just read too many novels set in the British Raj when I was growing up. Even when I was in junior high, I said I wanted to visit India someday. I dreamed of having an affair with a young officer who was constantly being called away..."

She placed the back of her hand against her forehead, shut her eyes and mimicked a distraught romance-novel heroine.

"...to ext*rem*ely hazardous duty in the Punjab."

She giggled. "If we bought a second wedding in India, do you suppose I'd get to ride down the aisle on a sacred cow?"

You might expect I'd instantly picture Marlise wrapped in a sari and rocking on the back of a white, dewlapped beast that ambled along an aisle of garlands toward a smoking altar.

Instead, I remembered my cousin Hal Junior waving from inside the fence at the airport in Vidalia last month, then hurrying off toward the hangar where he'd left his two-seater. In the lilac, late-summer twilight he looked as brisk and dapper as the young Air Force officer he'd been 30 years ago, when I'd begun to measure the distance between what he was and what I might become.

The other day my mother called to ask if Marlise and I could drive to Virginia for Thanksgiving. She said Dad had finally put new roofing on, and if we could come she'd get the ceiling in the upstairs bedroom repaired and the whole room re-papered.

"You know, the water leaking through from the roof has plumb *ruined* that ceiling," she said.

I do know. It was the same day Hal Junior flew off to South Carolina in his Piper Cub that Marlise threatened to move out of that bedroom to a motel, and to talk her out of it I had to promise I'd cut short our visit.

But when I told Mother I'd have to check with Marlise about a Thanksgiving trip, instead of remembering that furiously whispered scene beneath the strips of mildewed paper dangling from the ceiling, I remembered Hal Junior's station wagon pulling up in the driveway at Uncle Hal's house one Thanksgiving 20 or more years ago. I remembered how Hal Junior bounded up the brick steps and gave his mother a hug that, like everything he did, was strong, precise and swift. I remembered how his son, who was three years younger than I, greeted his grandparents in a way that mirrored his father's brisk gallantry. I remembered how the two little girls tumbled from the car and made a wild, tomboy dash for their grandfather. And I remembered the theatrically grand emergence of Hal Junior's wife, Briding, with a cigarette in an amber holder trailing from her hand.

But when I really do think of Hal Junior now—that is, when I choose to think of him, rather than have some image of him pop out of the middle of something else—I keep coming back to an evening in May four years ago, when I spent a couple of days with Hal Junior and his second wife, Hisako, at the cottage he'd bought on a little lake outside Pinckney, South Carolina.

I was still newspapering then. I'd been putting in long hours and had started to grow stale, and my city editor told me to vanish for a few days. Hal Junior had told me the previous Thanksgiving that he hoped I'd come when I could. So I called him and went.

It's the last evening I was there that I keep thinking of. Hal Junior grilled steaks, and while he was turning them, Hisako brought us green tea and tiny cakes of sweet, gluey rice wrapped in iridescent black seaweed. When we took the steaks inside, we set them on a plank-top table. Hal and Hisako had stripped and refinished the table and a pastry cupboard, both passed down from his father's home place outside Lynchburg.

It gave me a jolt when he opened that cupboard, an artifact of country sobriety, and I saw the liquor bottles and decanters and shakers. I knew that Hal never drank much himself. At Briding's parties, he'd always tended bar, and I supposed he still liked to mix drinks for guests. So instead of asking for a simple bourbon and water, I told him I'd like a Singapore Sling.

Not that I knew what a Singapore Sling was. I've long made it a point to know almost nothing about mixed drinks. I'm sure I'll learn more about them. Marlise will see to that.

Hal Junior laughed and slapped his knee, then slapped mine. "Boy, that takes about three kinds of liqueurs I don't have anymore!" he said. "Plus bitters, which I don't need either. Now, speaking as one country boy to another—how about Wild Turkey on the rocks?"

Later on, after it started to rain, we sat by a picture window and sipped the plum brandy Hisako had made and watched the glimmer of rain on the lake. I felt a vein of something fateful flowing sluggishly beneath the peace. Then Hal asked Hisako if she'd play something on her flute.

I expected a flute of lacquered, whiskey-colored bamboo, but instead she brought a conventional metal flute wrapped in green felt. Hal told her the Japanese name of the song he wanted to hear. Then she played it, and I told her it sounded sad. And she said no, it was not so sad a song, it was just that the Japanese tonal system is quite different.

That's all. Just the evening and the rain and the deep, throat-haunting taste of the brandy, and the slow vein of fate beneath the peace, and the song I had thought must be sad. I have no excuse to dwell on that memory, not when I have three fall classes to teach, no lesson plans prepared and Marlise on my neck about the shoes I'm supposed to wear for the wedding. Yet I think of that evening more and more.

~ * ~

Hal Junior and I were both drilled in the notion we should adopt our grandfather's life as a template for our own. Our mothers saw to that.

Their father had ascended from a rustic upbringing to the county school superintendency. That took him and his bride to Vidalia, where Aunt Charlotte, a boy who died in infancy, and finally my mother, were born. Grandfather was superintendent for nearly 20 years. Then he came back to the home place and served for a decade as principal of one of the rural schools that, as superintendent, he'd labored to build. Finally, he left school work and spent the rest of his life farming and lumbering and moodily dreaming of land deals in Canada, where he lost some thousands of dollars on the purchase of alleged wheat land that turned out to be afflicted with permafrost.

When Grandfather moved back to the farm, Charlotte, whom we called Chig, was finishing college, and my mother was still in elementary school. Aunt Chig already had behind her a girlhood that had flowered into popularity among the set of young people in Vidalia who had money and traveled and drank liquor and drove expensive cars. Not that Aunt Chig did any of those things. The first time her father found her shuffling a deck of playing cards, he snatched them up and threw them in the fireplace. But she was pretty and vivacious, she had a jolly dwarfish voice and a warm, sudden cackle of laughter. Vidalia was a small enough town in those days for the social orbit of church benefits and card parties in sober parlors (her father soon relented on card playing) to intersect with the cycle of soirees and debuts at the mansions. And once certain assurances were passed, her father let her go to the mansions, too.

By the time she was 21, Aunt Chig had proposals of marriage from Hal Benning, who had just enough money to pay his way through business college in Lynchburg, and from a young lawyer who had plenty of money and every prospect of getting more. Before she had to choose, the young lawyer was killed in a car accident in Richmond.

Uncle Hal never did get much money, but he found in 1933 that with what he'd saved he could build a house mortgage-free in the country on the lot Chig's father had given them. Later on, Mother got the home place simply because she still lived there and neither sister wanted to divide the property. When I was growing up, Uncle Hal and Aunt Chig were our only white neighbors within half a mile.

My grandparents, once they'd returned to the country, lapsed into country ways, and it was as a country girl that Mother grew up. Uncle Hal and Aunt Chig, however, kept their city ties intact. Thanks to Aunt Chig's girlhood popularity, they retained a place on the fringes of that level of Vidalia society that was as high as you could get without passing from the genteel into something else, something that had to do with weekend polo matches and flights of bootlegged Canadian whiskey and with minor film starlets who arrived in town wearing imitation mink and left wearing real chinchilla. Through his parents, Hal Junior acquired a taste for moneyed gentility, too.

Aunt Chig arranged for Hal Junior to attend Sedgewick High School in the city. Uncle Hal's place of work (he was house accountant for a soft drink bottling plant) was near the school. Until Hal was old enough to drive a jalopy, he rode to Sedgewick with his father.

Sedgewick High was a public school, but in those days in the South, the public schools in the wealthy sections of cities got the best of everything. If wealthy white families in a town like Vidalia decided to make a degree from their local public high school as good as a degree from any private school in the state, that school would rapidly acquire the commensurate faculty, tennis and soccer teams and aura of snobbery. Sedgewick was such a school, and in Vidalia nearly all the wealthy families sent their children there. Mother told me Grandfather's tenure as superintendent was cut short after he'd spent years prodding the school board to redirect some of its public funding from Sedgewick to the county's other high schools, including the single, overcrowded school that served Black children. In his view, Sedgewick High had all the resources it needed, and then some.

After Hal Junior enrolled at Sedgewick, there was a scene between Aunt Chig and Grandfather. The old man had started his career, about the turn of the century, teaching all the high school grades in a village nine miles from the farm. Every Sunday afternoon he bicycled from the farm to a rooming house in the village, and every Friday night he bicycled home. If the roads were muddy, he would slog the distance on foot.

Aunt Chig told me how, when he was superintendent, he had loved to ride by buggy out to the sturdy little brick schools that, under his supervision, were springing up all over the county. The schools were nearly identical, each with a white-clapboard tower capped by a triangular green cupola that housed the bell. Aunt Chig had often gone with him. She told me that sometimes they had to turn back, or the buggy would have gotten mired in churned red clay.

Mother told me what she knew of the scene between Grandfather and Aunt Chig. He asked Chig flatly why Cartersville School wasn't good enough for Hal Junior. Cartersville, like every other county school outside Vidalia at that time, was built under Grandfather's superintendency. It was one of the schools they'd watched struggling up out of the mud when they'd ride out by buggy. It was also the school where Grandfather had concluded his career with ten years as its principal. Grandfather asked Chig whose idea it was that Hal Junior attend Sedgewick, and she said Hal Junior himself had brought it up.

I think Grandfather might have left it at that, if Chig hadn't blurted something like, "Don't you want him to have the best education possible?" And the old man shot back at her, "The best education possible is to learn who you are, where you came from, and where you ought to go. Once you forget that, all the fancy schooling and fancy friends in the world won't help you remember it."

In the fall of 1941, Hal Junior went to Sedgewick High. He made plenty of friends there, some of them from families that owned sports cars and both beach and mountain cottages and memberships in the Sheffield Country Club. He got to ride in the sports cars, and he got to spend long weekends and whole weeks of summer vacation at the cottages. He went to parties at the country club, and to wedding receptions for his friends' older brothers and sisters. Also, he made a good, light but very fast halfback on the Sedgewick High School football team.

One of his school friends arranged a summer job for him at a hotel in a resort town in West Virginia. Though he was underage, it turned out his main duty was serving customers at the hotel's bar—something he told his parents only years later.

He must have learned a lot about mixing drinks that summer. What he learned served him well later on, when he tended bar at the parties Briding gave in the big, white-columned houses Briding insisted he buy.

Those few months in West Virginia led to another set-to, this time between Hal Junior and his grandfather. I was well into my teens when my mother fleshed out that story for me.

Hal Junior came home from the resort wearing the sort of white slacks and white shoes he must have seen rich men wearing at wrought-iron tables on the hotel terrace. He arrived in a car driven by the friend who'd gotten him the job. The friend's family had provided Hal a room in their summer home at the resort. Hal and his friend stopped first at the old farmhouse down the hill from his own home, so that he could give his grandparents a pair of tinted, hand-blown vases from a glass factory in Kentucky.

That was the summer after my mother married. Dad was laying telephone cable for a division headquarters unit in France, and Mom was living at the farm.

She said she was on the porch reading and Grandfather was out at the road putting a coat of paint on the mailbox post when Hal Junior and his friend pulled into the driveway in a sports car with the top down. Gus, the Black hired man, was across the road at the barn, shoveling out the horse stall and putting in fresh straw. Grandfather didn't need the horse for plowing any more, but Gus still needed a horse or mule to pull the tobacco sled, and Grandfather liked to hitch up the horse and give hayrides to the children at the church.

"That was a locust summer, I believe," Mother said. "Anyway, there were right many bugs stuck to their windshield, and you know you don't usually hit so many bugs driving through the mountains. Those boys' faces were all windburned on top of their tan, and their hair was cut long and waved out by the wind. And then they stepped out wearing those white pants and shoes. If a chariot had swooped down from the sky and a young Greek god had stepped out of it, he wouldn't have had a patch on either one of them.

"Papa straightened up from the paint bucket and gave them a hard, studying look, the way he might study a prize hog at the fair, picking out its points. The boys went out to the mailbox and talked to him a while. Then Papa went back to painting, and Hal Junior got the present he'd brought out of the car, and the boys came on into the house.

"Mama and I could see right away that something had happened out there. Hal Junior acted cheerful enough, but his eyes had a funny, glittery look in them, like he'd been kicked from a quarter he'd never expected to get kicked from. The other boy was kind of quiet, and he kept smiling a tight little smile that bared about four upper teeth. He had little knots of muscle high on his cheeks from keeping his face set in that squirrel-smile all the time.

"After they'd gone on up the hill to Hal and Chig's, Papa came in from painting, and Mama asked him what could have upset Hal Junior. And Papa blinked at her in that slow, heavy-lidded way he had when he got old. And then he said, 'I told them they oughtn't to stand too close to me, or they might get paint on their pants. He told me they were going to say hello to Gus, and I said they oughtn't to do that, or they might get manure on their shoes. I told Hal to be sure to come back when he'd changed into the kind of pants and shoes you can walk around on a farm in, if he still owned any of that kind.'

"And Mama said, 'Why, shame on you for embarrassing him like that! Your own grandson!'

"And Papa blinked at her, with one eyelid coming up a little slower than the other, and his mouth drooping at one corner, from his stroke. Then he said, 'That's right. He's my grandson. If he hadn't been, I might have asked them where they left their ice cream wagon.'"

After she'd told me this story, my mother's gristle-tipped nose must have twitched. It always gave a single twitch, like a rabbit's sniff, before she said something that ought to be looked into before it is believed.

"I can't imagine any two boys who come from the same family and who grew up on the same hill being any more different than you and Hal Junior are," she said.

Either I didn't see the sniff or I was so sure she was right that I paid no attention to it. I heard loud and clear her unspoken message: I'd shown promise of hewing to the template her father had set, and Hal Junior, despite pursuing a military career of some distinction, had strayed from it.

If anyone had asked me then how Hal Junior and I differed, I'd have said: Well, he played football, and I've found out at the cost of a torn ligament that I'm no good at it. He had a lot of girlfriends. I had big-nosed Rose Talley in the seventh grade, who ran a coy finger over the knee of my corduroy pants and said she was sorry I got moved to the other side of the classroom, and so far that's been it. He had friends of both sexes who were beautiful and rich. My friends at Cartersville High are few, male, frog-faced and no wealthier than I. He was Mr. Everything, and (if I'd inherited my mother's rabbit-sniff, I'd have used it here) I'd give anything to be like him. If I couldn't make good grades and run a decent half-mile, I'd be Mr. Nothing.

But, as I said this, down at the bottom of my 16-year-old heart I'd think: Ha-ha, you curly-haired halfback! Like a prize falcon you chased the lure of wealth and glamor, and what was your reward? A raven-throated scold, huge columned houses that are alien to your blood and beyond your means, and the privilege of tending bar at your wife's parties! Which of us, Mr. Everything, has hewed closer to our grandfather's precepts? If his shade has blessings yet to bestow, which of us will reap them?

~ * ~

Just now Marlise called to tell me that this Saturday, she'll drive up from Springfield, pick me up and take me to a Florsheim's in Chicago where they have my size in the style shoes she wants me to wear at the wedding.

I'm afraid I lost my temper. I reminded her that last Saturday at the mall in Bloomington I found three pairs of shoes that would do fine, and only need her to come with me to pick the pair she likes best.

There was quite a pause. "Listen, Howard," she said finally. Her tone was not dulcet. "Daddy has gone to a lot of trouble, and you are *not* going to disappoint him."

She said her father had called the store where he advised his firm's junior partners to buy their shoes. The store had the right style in 12-B.

"It's the least you can do, after all he's giving us."

I said what he was giving us was the wedding, period. There was another pause. Then she said Daddy had already bought round-trip tickets for the two of us to New Delhi, and she hung up.

I wonder if Grandfather could've foreseen Marlise swaying on the back of a Brahma heifer?

~ * ~

When Hal Junior finished high school in 1945, he joined the Air Corps. He earned a commission as a bombardier, but by the time he finished training, there was no enemy left to bomb. He cross-trained as a transport plane pilot, then spent two years in Japan. Mother said there was something about a Japanese girl, but it never came to anything. Then the Air Force sent him to Charlottesville for a degree, and he missed another war. He had a way of missing wars. His military career spanned three wars, and he missed them all.

In my own early childhood, though, I knew nothing about the bits of Hal Junior's history that would later complicate my view of him. I knew only that I had an older cousin who had grown up in the brick house atop our hill, and who had embraced a life of risk by learning to fly airplanes. I remember a summer day before I was old enough for school when my mother and I were lying on a blanket in the yard outside our farmhouse. I watched an airplane pass through a gap in the clouds, and for a moment, the fuselage shone with an almost unbearable silvery brightness. A wing dipped, and I saw the flag on the tail. I asked if Hal Junior might be the pilot. "Sure," she said.

After college, he was stationed at Charleston, South Carolina. I think he asked to go there. And there I discern his fate picking up the thread.

He might have gone to Charleston expecting to find the life at the Sheffield Country Club raised to a higher power. What he did find was something quite different. What he'd known before was the status bestowed on industrialists and financiers, pretty much as a function of their wealth and in direct proportion to the amount of it. Its markers included sports cars and polo fields and open terraces of smooth, snugly fitted flagstones. The essential element was current wealth that was flaunted or—in the pursuit of still greater wealth—wielded as a weapon.

In Charleston, the rich he met rarely broached the subject of wealth, and never flaunted their own. They took him to hunt breakfasts and steeplechases, and in the evenings he found himself among figures that drifted wraithlike across elm-gloomed terraces where the stones were old and cracked and splotched with lichens. The wooden columns on the porches of the Vidalia rich had been smooth and gleaming with fresh paint. In Charleston, the verandahs had bulbous plaster pillars that were lumpy with generations' worth of patches beneath the whitewash. The life he found behind those pillars was a life of ease, certainly, but of ease from which the inky smell of cash had long since departed, ease so inbred that neither gain nor loss of wealth could affect its essence. To this ancient and settled ease of Charleston, Hal Junior succumbed.

But instead of marrying some soft-drawling incarnation of all that, he married Briding. That part I understand least, and in my current situation—one step short of an equally ill-chosen bondage—I find it rather important to try to understand.

Briding was from Greenville, Mississippi. When Hal Junior met her, she was summering with relatives in Charleston. (I, too, met Marlise in what in terms of my life's trajectory counted as a sort of mecca, grad school in Urbana.) The money in Briding's family was nearly as old as the money along the Charleston battery. Certainly, it was older than Vidalia money. (Urbana circa 1975 was awash in Seven Sisters PBKs, but Marlise's Northwestern *cum laude* seemed just enough for a country boy.) Briding might never do anything with her hands that would risk splitting her lacquered nails, but she could do a man's work with her tongue. (Ah, Grandfather!)

Usually on Thanksgiving Day, my parents and I would already be waiting at Uncle Hal's and Aunt Chig's house when Hal Junior's station wagon arrived. Briding would wait until the greetings of her husband and children were done, as if these were mere preliminaries. Then she would approach the brick steps with her eyelids aristocratically lowered and her arms half-lifted as if she were the hostess extending welcome.

She would sweep into the pine-paneled living room like Bacall entering a stage. When she reached the center of the room, she would throw back her head and close her eyes, as if she were about to sneeze. But what followed would be a great, hoarse cry of greeting, in which her voice would crack dramatically, giving an oogah-horn quality to the stressed syllables.

"Hello-o, hello-o! My, here you all a-are, and I know everything's lo-ong been ready, and don't you know these absolutely po-okey people from South Caroli-ina would be la-ate, while all of you sit here gro-oaning in the last stages of starva-ation? My he-eavens, I shall ne-ever understa-and how you Virginians can bear this horrid we-eather, you must be absolute po-olar bears!"

Until dinner was truly ready, we'd be treated to an hors d'oeuvre of Briding's rasping voice and Briding's cigarette smoke. Hal Junior and his son would go straight to the kitchen, and those of us who wanted to talk to them would go there, too. I wondered if they had to do that at their own home when Briding held court.

What I know of Briding's feelings toward Grandfather comes from Mother. She told me a few years ago, after Hal Junior got his divorce and married Hisako, and word got around that Briding had persuaded her children not to see him anymore.

"I wouldn't ever have given Briding credit for being very much in tune with what other people were thinking," Mother said. "But she seemed to pick up something from Papa that not even I could detect. You remember the time she just froze up in front of him, don't you?"

I didn't remember. I couldn't have been more than four years old at the time.

"Well, she was cawing along as usual. I used to say she reminded me of an Iowa crow lording it over birds that had to get their pickings off of one-horse farms. And Papa went to sleep. Dozed off right in front of her. Nobody but a half-deaf man could do that. It was just for a minute, but while he was asleep, he muttered a little. 'Brrr*uum*-hum-hum-hum,' like that. She went on about how divine or horrid something was, and just gave Papa an uneasy glance or two. Then Papa woke up, and that did it. His left eye opened a little before the right one did, and that just stopped her cold. One or both of his eyes must have conveyed in an instant what he really thought of her. When Papa got woken up properly, he just looked at her right kindly, not seeming to notice she'd stopped talking or that he had anything to do with it. But it took her several minutes to get her tongue working again, and even then it sounded like she'd sprained it a little.

"Vickie (Hal Junior's youngest sister) told me later that she'd gotten up in the middle of the night to see if she'd left her watch in the living room, and as she was passing the foot of the stairs she heard Briding. It sounded like her tongue had healed up fine. Briding said she wasn't in the habit of riding three hundred miles in freezing weather to have an old buzzard-eyed hick make a fool of her. The only thing that surprises or disappoints me about what Vickie heard is that Hal Junior didn't say a word. I could've told Briding she was talking about a man who'd hired himself out in hay-baling season to pay his university tuition, and then built schools that have served five generations and counting. I could've told her, too, that she needn't travel any farther than it took to glance in the mirror on her antique cherry wood dressing table in South Carolina to find the person most likely to make a fool of her. Vickie swore me to secrecy, and I've never even told Chig. But I see no reason now to keep that particular cat bagged up any longer."

~ * ~

I knew my grandfather only slightly. I remember his pale, doughy, lumpy-featured face, the sort of face I saw on a lot of old German farmers when I was in the Army. I remember the way his dim blue eyes glinted moistly behind matted white brows, and the way his right eyelid seemed to snag as it rose, and the right corner of his mouth drooped and quivered. I remember the braided hearing aid cord running from his shirt pocket to the plug in his ear, and his huge slow hands, the gray cotton work clothes he always wore around the house, the leaden heaviness of his step, the salty-leathery smell of age. I remember how uncomfortable and impatient I'd feel when he'd lift me onto his lap and read to me. He read in a phlegmy, nasal drone, and his ponderous old fingers fumbled and fumbled at each page. He was as huge-boned as a draft horse. Whenever I squirmed in his lap, I'd smack my head or elbow against massive bone.

He died before I was six. It was an April day, and Mother was moving some item of furniture from one room to another. Whatever it was, it was big, and she was lugging one piece of it at a time. She was passing through the hall when she saw him standing at the foot of the stairs with his hand on the banister.

"Doll?" he said, squinting at her. "Doll?" Then he fell backward, banging his head on the stairs, and he died. Doll was his pet name for my grandmother, dead five years before him.

I didn't know him well at all. Yet by the time I was grown, I believed I was his spiritual heir.

Lately I'm not so sure.

Like A Wary Blessing

~ * ~

Hal Junior spent a few years in Germany around the middle of his Air Force career, but he managed to spend most of the rest of it in South Carolina, at Charleston and Columbia. Once in a while, my parents and I would spend a holiday weekend at Hal Junior's. Mother would have gladly taken a pass when Hal Junior invited us, but my father would eagerly accept. He had grown up in a poor farm family in Mississippi, not far from Briding's hometown. As an assistant principal in one of the schools Grandfather had built, Dad liked to think he'd ascended a few rungs on the social ladder. The atmosphere of decaying opulence in any household where Briding presided seemed to bolster his self-regard.

But even as a child, I sensed the blight. The houses were always too big and too filled with Briding's commands and raucous laughter. There were too many ashtrays and all of them were overflowing with Briding's cigarettes. Hal Junior spent too much time smiling but tight-lipped behind a bar in the drawing room, while Briding held court with a steady stream of her friends. One morning I saw Hal Junior in his Air Force uniform—I think he was a captain then—cleaning up party trash before he drove to the base. As he set the glasses and coasters and napkins on a tray, I caught the baleful yet stoic cast of his gray eyes. I thought he looked like a servant in his own home.

Even as a child, I wondered how Hal Junior could afford the big houses with their fluted columns. He and Briding acquired a succession of these—two, at least in Charleston, and one in Columbia, where for a few years he was the ranking officer in the university's Air Force ROTC program. I wondered why there seemed to be so little of Hal Junior himself in the things he bought—the houses, the horses he didn't ride, the liquor he didn't drink, the private schools and riding lessons for his children. I wondered why he wanted any of it.

Later on, it became clear that Hal Junior didn't want all that quite as much as he'd once believed he did. I knew too, though, from the baleful but determined light in his eyes, that no matter how that life had soured for him, he'd live it out for whatever he felt to be the term of his commitment.

After I finished college, I took a job writing obituaries for the *Vidalia Sun*. It took a while for the draft board to yank my student deferment and schedule me for a physical. Hal Junior came up for a few days that summer to help his parents with some chore—I think it was ridding their home of a mouse infestation. I hadn't known he was there until a morning when I was tacking up some loose barbed wire on the pen where we kept our beef calf, and he waved at me from his parents' screen porch.

I put down my hammer and walked up the hill. He brought out two bottles of Dr Pepper and we sat on the porch and drank them. There were always plenty of Dr Peppers in that house, since Uncle Hal worked at the bottling plant. I told Hal Junior I planned to play up my knee injury from high school football in a bid for a draft exemption. He set down his Dr Pepper on a glass-topped table and gave me a long look and said, "Howie, you just do what you believe's right. But try to think of what our grandfather would do."

It didn't occur to me just then that military service had never been an issue for Grandfather. He'd been too old for the draft in 1917. It didn't occur to me either to mention that Hal Junior himself had never spent a day in combat and seemed to have no interest in serving in Vietnam.

During my draft physical, I didn't mention my knee injury. I spent a year in Vietnam teaching English to Vietnamese pilot trainees, then a year and a half in Germany as a photo interpreter. We peered through stereoscopes at film shot from military aircraft flying to and from Berlin over communist territory. We identified and counted all weaponry visible on the film—artillery, tanks, aircraft, military vehicles of any kind—and reported those tallies to American and allied recipients who had a need to know, or thought they did. Those six months at the *Sun* were an ideal priming for Army life, which all turned out to be very much better than writing obituaries.

While I was in Germany, I got a letter from Mother saying Hal Junior had retired at the rank of lieutenant colonel. He'd bought an interest in a pilot training school and was going to teach there while he studied for a real estate license.

Like A Wary Blessing

~ * ~

Marlise came into my office half an hour ago. While she was here, I shuffled books and papers on my desk, trying to hide the pages of this history.

She'd driven to campus from the legislative staff building in Springfield. She wore a bright scarf looped around her neck and turned out artfully on her shoulder. She's taken to wearing bright scarves since she went to work for Representative Simon Redonzo.

"I guess I've been acting like a real bitch," she said, and she giggled. I used to find that giggle disarming.

"It's just that this wedding makes me so *nervous*," she said. "I'd almost rather we ran off to a j.p. in—where was it you said kids in Virginia run off to get married?"

"South Carolina," I said. "Only some of them with different ideas run off to Illinois."

"Honestly, Howard, I won't be like this once we're married."

I didn't ask her what she'd be like once we're married. Instead, I fell to studying her clothes.

A few months ago, she told me she spends a hundred dollars a month on clothes. I told her I didn't spend a hundred dollars a year on clothes. She said, well, I wasn't a woman working for Simon Redonzo.

Mr. Redonzo is a gentleman with large teeth. He owns a block of tenements in Chicago, and he routinely patches them up one step ahead of the building inspectors. He collects Spanish wooden crucifixes and manger tableaux, and he imports his household servants from the Philippines.

Mr. Redonzo has fashioned a political career by proving to his Highland Park constituents that liberal views, if carefully selected, can be painless. Recently Marlise wrote a press handout in which Mr. Redonzo advocates natural gas furnaces in public housing.

I suggested to Marlise that Mr. Redonzo equip his tenements with natural gas heating too, so his tenants wouldn't get scalded or maimed the next time their steam pipes burst or their kerosene heaters blow up. She said that sometimes I get surly.

She said Daddy and Mr. Redonzo are friends. I wonder how I'd skipped learning that. I did know that Daddy's firm represents Mr. Redonzo's business interests. On a whim, using public records, I found those interests include a silent partnership in a natural gas distribution company.

Mr. Redonzo adds to the Latin flavor of his business and legislative offices by urging his female employees to wear glossy lipstick and clothes of the colors to be found in a parrot's tail. When I met Marlise at grad school, she wore jeans and her brother's old long-sleeved shirts. They struck me as being the kind of clothes you could walk around on a farm in.

Now, in the outfits that cost a hundred dollars a month, she falls somewhere between Junior League president and Miami Beach streetwalker.

Before she left a few minutes ago, Marlise put her hand on mine. I noticed her nails were done in the same hue as her lips. It's the color of the flesh inside a well-chilled morgue drawer, but much glossier.

"Promise you're not angry?" she said.

I promised, and it was true. Even my viscera know it's too late for anger.

She yielded up to me lips the hue of glittering death. Then she said she'd pick me up at 11 Saturday to go to Chicago for the shoes.

~ * ~

Hal Junior left Briding a couple of years after he retired from the Air Force, and just a few months after his youngest daughter entered college. He skipped the Thanksgiving gathering at Aunt Chig's. By Easter he'd married Hisako. He'd met her at the pilot training school, where she kept books. Her husband had been killed while piloting an Army helicopter in Vietnam. Her children, two tall, quiet boys whose gangling arms contrasted oddly with their compact oriental faces, spent nine months of the year with grandparents in Missouri.

Briding persuaded her own children to stop seeing Hal Junior as soon as she learned he'd married a woman of color.

Hal Junior signed on with a real estate firm in Pinckney. I suppose moving there made things less awkward, since Briding still lived in Columbia.

Thereafter, when Hal Junior came to Virginia at Thanksgiving, he drove a melon-green Austin-Healey. Hisako would bring a fruitcake she'd made with her plum brandy.

Aunt Chig would always receive the fruitcake with a show of surprise. "Why, *thank* you, Hisako!" she'd say. "My land, you make the best fruitcakes. Wherever did you learn to make such wonderful holiday things?"

"Oh, no," Hisako would say softly, with her eyes downcast. "It is so simple. Really, I am ashamed to bring you so simple a thing."

At some point during each of these holiday visits, Uncle Hal would pluck at Hisako's arm. "If you don't mind sneaking off with an old man, I've got something I'd like to show you," he'd tell her in a stage whisper.

They'd go to the basement where, following her directions, he was making fruit brandies. Presently we'd see them from the living room window, as they inspected Uncle Hal's fruit trees and arbor. There was a quietly funny, formal quality about the two of them on these expeditions—the wiry, beaming old man and the slim, dark-haired woman following him along the aisle of barren fruit trees with her eyes lowered and her feet moving in a demure shuffle.

After Briding's exit, I began to scan Hal Junior for signs of regeneration. And I did detect traces of what Mother called "the old Hal Junior."

But if something of the old Hal Junior had returned, the intervening one had left its mark. He no longer had to go to the kitchen to make himself heard. Still, out of habit I suppose, he did go there. His voice had shed its quality of steely self-control, but now it was often raised in pointless dispute about football teams, tax laws, the evils of welfare and busing. Bigotry had always been Briding's long suit, not Hal Junior's. But after his marriage to Hisako, his allusions to the Black race took on real virulence. His eyes had lost the baleful glint, but what replaced it was a feverish emptiness, as if he were straining to reach back beyond the years of stoic denial and finding there was nothing left to retrieve.

It was five years ago that Hal Junior told me at the family's Thanksgiving gathering that he felt his life had been a waste. That was the year after Uncle Hal died—he dropped dead while square-dancing with Aunt Chig at the county fair—and half a year before I visited Hal Junior and Hisako in Pinckney.

It was after dinner, and except for Hal Junior and me, the kitchen was empty. He sat on a low wall cupboard with his small loafers not quite touching the floor. He got from his father a facility for perching on scant surfaces.

"A man does his best," he said, the old baleful light rekindling in his eyes. "He sets himself a few ideals and tries to live them out. He makes his mistakes—but by golly, he lives those out too, when he might have tucked his tail and run from them. He sets his own happiness aside until he's given his kids the right kind of start in life. And for what?" He spread his arms like Job exhibiting his boil-covered nakedness. "For what?"

When I went to Pinckney the next spring, I'd been back at the *Sun* as a reporter for about four years. Though I didn't quite know it yet, I was poised for flight from Vidalia. The following September, I left for grad school in Urbana.

In some way that I still can't put my finger on, that visit to Pinckney was a leave-taking. It certainly wasn't a matter of my rising arc intersecting his falling one. I didn't feel especially on the way up. At any rate, I knew my cresting-out point wasn't likely to be very high above the *Vidalia Sun*. And even taking into account his lament a few months earlier while perched on the kitchen cabinet in the house where he'd grown up, there was no reason to think of Hal Junior as decidedly on the way down.

I found it important not to have to think of him as on the way down. I'd begun to feel his course through life somehow prefigured my own.

The drive to Pinckney took two hours longer than I'd planned. I seem always to have that problem when I travel South, as if there were some hypnotic quality about the region, even on a map, that keeps me from focusing on actual distances. It was nearly midnight when I reached the Pinckney turnoff. Away from the Interstate, the pines seemed sparser and more ragged, the moonlit sand chalkier. By the time I reached the darkened cottage and glimpsed the tiny pier fingering into the invisible lake, I felt I'd reached some land's end.

I'd heard some whispered bitterness, from Vickie I think it was, about the alimony Hal Junior had to pay. Whenever I hear the word alimony now, I see that tiny cottage amid scrub-covered dunes; I can see Hal Junior's freckled shoulders and the turned-down swabby's cap shielding the back of his neck as he lay sunning on the rotting gray boards of that miserable pier.

Yet it seemed to me that in Hisako and that cottage, Hal Junior had stumbled on a rare sort of peace. Hisako loved that little house, loved every corner of it. She flashed about the cottage constantly on her flat-soled, splay-toed bare feet. When she worked at the stove, she seemed to hook those strong brown toes right down into the tile. Love of her house was there even in the way she wielded a wooden spoon as she made soup.

Pinckney was a microcosm of things Southern. One of its faces was that of a dreary mill town. There was a somnolent, oak-lined avenue where the oldest families lived. Though the town had little to commend it as a resort, Northern industrialists of the horsey sort had built winter homes there. The big event of that set was a race of two-year-olds, horses that would later run at the great tracks in Kentucky.

One evening, Hal Junior drove us slowly past the columned houses and the broad lawns with their Black-faced, grinning, cast-iron coachmen, and past the mostly empty stables. The three big equestrian events, two races and a steeplechase, had wrapped up the month before. Hal Junior talked about the gala doings surrounding the races, and about the market values of the homes. His eyes glittered like a child's eyes lit by the tawdry lights of a carnival.

"I don't see anything wonderful about houses so big and fine," Hisako said. Her voice sounded shaky and spiteful. "In Japan, we say it is bad breeding to show off your wealth like that."

Hal Junior turned toward her with his eyebrows arched. Then a couple of ugly things happened.

"Perhaps you've noticed that you're not *in* Japan now," he said. And with her eyes fleeing in a baffled rush, Hisako shrank into a corner of the back seat.

The other ugly thing was my own tremor of glee that she'd been put in her place.

On the drive home to Virginia, I thought about how Hal had sort of tagged me with that bullying remark, knowing I'd endorse it, if only by my silence.

And then I thought back to a night when, working late at the *Sun*, I'd wandered into the newspaper's morgue and pulled out the manila envelope stuffed with clippings about my grandfather. The paper's librarian had photocopied old clippings of local interest, and I found a feature story from 1932, after Grandfather had been ousted as superintendent. It mentioned the hayrides he'd given children at our church. It said he'd also given a hayride to children at the nearby Black church, some of them descendants of people who'd "once worked for the family."

I'd counted backward by the likely life spans of those children's parents and grandparents until I reached 1865. Then I'd stood there, alone in the morgue beneath a buzzing fluorescent light, wondering whether for my grandfather, the hayride for those Black children was purely an act of generosity and atonement. Perhaps, I thought, it had instead been a feeble "up yours" by an embittered old man, directed at the school board members who'd replaced him after he'd badgered them for years to equalize funding across all county schools. My mother had told me the board had also stiffed him when he asked them to buy at least some new textbooks for the Black schools, rather than send them only books that were tattered and out of date after years of use at the white schools. But I never found independent evidence he'd done that.

Not knowing which mix of motives fit the case of that old man gently slapping the reins against Queenie's rump while grandchildren of his family's slaves romped across the loose hay in the wagon bed behind him, I couldn't tell whether that vision of my grandfather should make me feel proud, mortified or both.

I couldn't use as a template for my own life a man I barely knew. If any man could serve that purpose, he'd have to be an ongoing presence in my life. My father, then? My father taught me the value of focused effort, but in his telling, that value always traced back to the days in his youth when he'd crawled in blistering heat between two rows of cotton plants, picking from both rows at once. As a model for something more than stubborn plodding, I'd needed more than my father could offer. I'd needed someone I'd once envisioned piloting his silvery vessel through a sunlit patch between clouds. Someone who'd given his wings a little waggle intended just for me.

~ * ~

Last March, Mr. Redonzo sent Marlise to a week-long PR seminar in Charleston. I asked her later how she liked junketing on money Mr. Redonzo's tenants could have used to buy rat poison. She bridled at that, and said every penny came from tax funds.

The day the seminar ended, Hal Junior drove down and took her to Pinckney for the weekend. The season among the horsey set was in full swing then, and Hal Junior saw to it that Marlise was well watered.

I'd briefed her on his history. She came back babbling about horses and some actual, fleshly DuPont she'd met in Pinckney, but curiously silent about Hal. I wondered if he'd made a pass at her and felt oddly pleased at the thought.

Finally, she said, "It does seem a shame, doesn't it?"

Her voice had that bright, otherworldly tone certain women use when they want to convey some nasty idea without letting a word of it soil their lips.

"What does?" I said.

"That he should give up all that for—you know."

"Give up all what? And for what?"

"Well, it simply looks like—I mean, there's no accounting for tastes."

"For God's sake, Marlise, I don't know what you're talking about."

Actually, I was pretty sure I did know, and what infuriated me was her assurance that I would know. By "there's no accounting for tastes," she could only mean Hisako.

The fair breeze of that attitude must have fanned Hal Junior quite often in Pinckney. Or maybe all that was needed was some current of it in himself.

July was the first time I'd seen Aunt Chig since she'd sold her house and moved into an apartment at the new Presbyterian Home in Vidalia. There was the usual quota of lost-looking old shells drifting along the halls, but Aunt Chig bustled about chattering and laughing like a bubbly freshman in a dorm. The pouched flesh beneath her eyes stuck to her glasses and gave her an eager, popeyed look.

When she said Hal Junior was going to fly up, I asked if Hisako would come with him.

"No-o-o," she said, as if the word were very fragile and mustn't be let drop. "No, I don't think she *will* come."

Hal Junior flew in at two in the afternoon, and he flew out again before eight. His sister Connie drove him to her house from the airport. Then she brought Hal Junior and two of her own children to Aunt Chig's apartment, where his mother, Marlise, Vickie and I were waiting for him. The gathering was so filled with breezy chatter, and Hal Junior's purpose was so clearly to keep it that way, that I gave up the idea of talking seriously with him.

I couldn't have said what I thought we needed to talk about. But ever since I'd heard he was coming, I'd felt that something of moment had to pass between us.

"How's Hisako?" I blurted finally. "Too busy at home to come up, I guess."

There was silence for about the time it would take a pariah dog to slink through the room.

"Hisako's just fine, last I heard," Hal said evenly. "Hey, now what about your wedding plans?"

I left that to Marlise. I noted that "Daddy" figured prominently in our wedding plans. Somehow "Howard's promotion" and "trip to someplace exotic" and "bid on a house" had gotten into them, too.

Finally, Hal stood and said, "I'm sorry to break up the party, chillun. But I've got to be in the air before sundown. So, zip-zip! Zip-zip!"

Aunt Chig had been able to keep her big Pontiac at the Presbyterian home. We all crowded into it, and Aunt Chig asked me to drive. When Hal had kissed his mother and sisters, I walked behind him to the gate. He pressed the button of a speaker there and said, "This is Hal Benning, and I need to come in to get to my plane, please." In his taut, over-courteous tone, I could hear how badly he wanted to get away.

Before the gate opened, he turned to me.

"I wish all the best for you, Howie," he said. "But however it works out, you just make the best of it, you hear?"

"I'll do that, for sure," I said. "No reason to think it won't work out, is there?"

He pinned my eye, and something flew from his eye to mine. Probably it flew right back from my eye to his. And I felt that pariah dog slink through my gut.

"Just you remember whose grandson you are," he said. "Remember that, and I know you'll do the right thing."

Later Vickie told me. Vickie was never beautiful, but at 42 she's getting close. Age has purged her of freckles, rounded her figure and given her deep, dramatic eyes to go with her bony nose. Nowadays she could pass for an atavistic granddaughter of the Ptolemies.

That morning I'd dropped off Marlise at a mall in town, then driven to Vickie's apartment. It's been a couple of years since Vickie divorced her husband. He was a saxophone-tootling, tape-pirating lout who plummeted from the Duke glee club to the Bunny Bread delivery fleet to, finally, complete unemployment. En route, he lost Vickie's house and the land Uncle Hal had given them to build it on, while Vickie slaved on as a first-grade teacher and, during all vacations, as a clothing store clerk.

"Did you know Hal and Hisako had separated?" Vickie said.

"No," I said. "Oh, hell."

"I thought you didn't."

Vickie loves plants that hang in rope baskets from the ceiling. There was one of them between us. On one side, the plant's tendrils trailed nearly to the floor.

"Where did she go?" I said. "Missouri?"

"No, she's still living at the house on the lake. Hal's moved into an apartment in Pinckney, I think. You saw how he acted the other night, like he wanted to hurry his visit along as smoothly as he could and then get away? Well, about a month ago, Mama wrote him a real scorcher of a letter about his marriage—about both his marriages. She told me about it after she'd sent it, and I just said, 'Oh, Mother!' Because I knew it was the wrong thing to do, especially now. I know he feels guilty enough already, without having Mama light into him. But Mama always expected the world of him, and I guess it's too much to ask her to keep quiet about things now."

Vickie absently plucked some yellowed leaves off a tendril of the plant. One leaf dropped from her fingers and, falling obliquely through sunlight, whirled like a tiny golden whirligig.

"Do you know what brought it on?" I said.

She shredded the dead leaves into an ashtray. "In a way, I think I do. You know, Hisako never could mix in the high society down there. She had no taste for it, and I'm sure a lot of those people, Briding's sort of people, wouldn't have accepted her. All she wanted was to be at home with him. But that could never be all that Hal Junior would want."

So that was it. The moth drawn again to the flame.

"I don't think there's any other woman," Vickie said. "But I've told you all I really know."

~ * ~

I just dropped Marlise off beside her car in my apartment parking lot. She hopped out without a word and drove off toward Springfield. She drove up here this morning, planning to take me to Chicago to get the shoes, but I insisted we take my car instead. I just craved a little control over my destiny, or the illusion of it. Now, having run that gauntlet of industrial stink to get them, I can say with faint satisfaction that the shoes fit and have a fine, lustrous grain. But they wouldn't do to walk around a farm in.

In Chicago, we stopped by Daddy's office downtown. Daddy has stubby fingers which he spreads on his desk and occasionally scans with his eyes as if he were counting the checkers he has left on the board. I thanked him for the privilege of driving 300 miles round-trip to buy shoes I'll wear once.

While I drove back here, I tried to tell Marlise a few things. Tactfully. Too tactfully for her to notice at first. She was working with a pocket calculator and the notes she's made at real estate offices. She computed probable mortgage terms on some houses in the $80,000 bracket. She compared those with what I'll earn once I make assistant prof, plus what she intends to get next year from Simon Redonzo. She kept coming up with sizable figures called X. These were amounts we'd be short on each house if we continued to eat and to buy the sort of clothes that please Mr. Redonzo. I fear these figures called X will in time become associated with either Daddy's largesse or, *mirabile dictu*, my entry into the business world.

I told her to quit or she'd make herself carsick. She did quit when it was getting dark. Then all I'd said seemed to sink in at once.

"Do you mean," she said in a wavering tone, "that after all your promises, and after all these preparations (she may actually have thumped the shoebox here), you intend to call the wedding off?"

"I'm simply saying you should ask yourself again whether this is for the best, whether it's likely to last," I said. "As long as marrying me is what you want, my promise is as good as money in the bank."

I'm afraid that clinched it. All of it. The wedding on Daddy's dime, the flight to New Delhi, where maybe a pariah dog and I can swap notes on our shared status. Because I'm sure Marlise will never relinquish anything as good as money in the bank.

And now I think I know what it is that keeps pulling me back to that last evening at Hal Junior's cottage by the lake.

It's the song Hisako played. Those liquid minor notes that sounded so like the awry melody of the years, composed to a tonal system we never foresaw. The song that she said was really not so sad.

Now I know: It was sad, all right. Sadder yet than memory. Sad beyond all regret.

Harry and the Ugly Rug

We all know Harry Waters's kind, if we have grown up in an American town of the proper size. They can be found at post office corners—gassed veterans of the Argonne, shell-shocked scalers of Monte Casino—ranting of Armageddon between turns at directing traffic. Not that Harry had ever been gassed or shell-shocked. His limbs were intact and sound, his gaze steady and unclouded. You would have to know Harry quite well before his craziness would glimmer forth like a tiny and distant glint of gold on a dusty Asian road.

Harry was a retired Air Force major, a Korean War fighter pilot with battle ribbons to his credit. Legend had it he'd asked to be taken off flight status in Korea after he'd killed a peasant family because he didn't release the trigger fast enough after he'd strafed a column of Inmun Gun infantry. He lived alone in a village near his last duty station, an air base in the German Rhineland.

Some who'd observed Harry's drinking bouts at the officers' club claimed that, when sufficiently soused, he'd rant about the family he'd killed. He'd say that when he took a second, lower pass over the site, he could see that one of the dead was a girl who wore a gold ring. And he pledged to her he'd marry none else.

~ * ~

One day when Harry came home from a visit to the Mainz cathedral, he found an old, rolled-up carpet on the landing outside his apartment door.

He was feeling depressed. He had liked the baroque statuary inside the cathedral, but the exterior depressed him utterly. It was such a hodgepodge, for one thing. With its style-less, planless assemblage of spires and buttresses, and its two huge unfinished towers, it resembled a horribly arthritic horned toad.

But that was not the worst. The worst was the color. The native red sandstone was used to construct every sort of building in Mainz. But to build a cathedral of it seemed to him unthinkable.

Yet there it was. It would have been laughable if it were not so awful. When finally he fled from it, he felt it was gliding after him: a galleon rigged by a madman, the color of dried blood on dust.

When he found the rug outside his door, Harry ran down the three flights of stairs and buzzed at his landlady's door. He heard Frau Link's heavy, slippered tread, and he trembled.

"Ah, Herr Waters!" Frau Link said before the door was half open. He was, it was clear, expected.

"Der Teppich!" Harry blurted.

"Ah, der Teppich!" she said. *"Der ist ja von mir!"* Her smile had nothing to do with the carpet, and briefly Harry wondered if black widow spiders ever smile. *"Ich hab' ein Pfirsiche Kuchen gemacht!"*

With peach Kuchen plastered to the roof of his mouth, and a gooey foreboding lodged in the ventricles of his heart, Harry climbed the stairs to his door. If the rug was from Frau Link, he would have to use it. In his life of eternal, never-to-be-consummated betrothal, Harry had learned this inviolable rule: until it becomes absolutely necessary and the route of escape is clear, never disappoint a widow.

So with a pasty, peach-flavored dread caked like centuries of candle smoke on the vaulted ceiling of his soul, Harry dragged the heavy carpet into his bedroom. (She hauled it up three flights by herself? Never cross that woman!) He unrolled one edge of it.

Instantly he rolled it up again in horror.

He pulled his big wardrobe away from the wall and heaved the carpet behind it. When he pushed the *Schrank* back into place, the carpet was hidden behind it.

Harry spent the rest of the afternoon in feverish housekeeping activity. The military passion for spotless order had never really taken with Harry. But, as now, it came back to him in fits and seizures. He washed the dishes that had overflowed his sink. For the first time in months, he scrubbed the ring off his bathtub, using a copper scouring pad. When he realized the pad was scratching the porcelain, he scrubbed even harder, gritting his teeth and muttering, "Thus to those who would intrude upon my vow!" He swept the cigar ash, eraser dust and pencil shavings from behind his desk, and even washed his ash tray. He mopped his tiny kitchen and washed every window in the place. Finally, he spread cleanser in the kitchen and bathroom sinks, on the kitchen table and counter and the toilet bowl and scrubbed them until they gleamed and were as fresh as all outdoors.

But he could not rid his dwelling of the taint that had come into it.

That very night, it seemed to him later, the carpet had begun to smell.

He could not admit it at first. He told himself it was a dead animal on a nearby street, or vapors wafted from a miles-distant chemical plant.

But it was the rug. Soon there could be no question of it. The odor grew stronger, and it got into the clothes inside his *Schrank*.

Something was dead or dying inside that rolled-up carpet. He didn't dare guess at what it might be.

Already it was late September. On October first, Frau Link would come into the apartment to open the valves of his radiators. As per his bilingual contract. Heat: October 1 to April 1. Frau Link, a woman of broad *Plattdeutsch* wit and tastes, had a radiator key of unique design.

Punctually on October first, Frau Link would perform the dance of postharvest. The wheat is in the granary, oh gleaner. Who, when snow sweeps through the stubble like the sands of a transposed Sahara—who shall warm thy bed? The *Apfelwoi* is in the *Kellar* keg. Who, oh harvester and hunter—who shall line thy flight boots with the pelt of the *Kaninchen*?

In the dance of postharvest, Frau Link's autumnal, bumper-crop form swayed enticingly behind three veils, *Apfelwoi, Aprikot Kuchen und Handkäse*. The apple wine and onion-sprinkled hand cheese gave him the runs. The *Kuchen,* despite the apricots, stopped him up again like so much putty. Frau Link offered him the flow and ebb of the seasons themselves: the gushing bounty, and the dry, pinched season of brooding and discontent.

On the last day of September, when his overwrought senses transformed the mellifluous odor of death inside that carpet into essence of *Handkäse,* Harry pulled the carpet out from behind the *Schrank* and, braced for the worst, threw it open across his bedroom floor.

In a flash, Harry saw the genesis of that rug. The rugmaker had gazed at the Mainz cathedral until he had absorbed the very shape, pattern and color of madness. Then he had rushed home and created his master work in a burst of frenzied energy.

...creatures like stingrays with petal fins, swimming through a cave-painting sea of blood...

...pinch-mouthed tulip shapes, lurid blossoms blooming in the tulips' inner darkness, stamens squeezing outward to drink of that bloody tint...

...curling nightshade tendrils, connecting the poisonous blooms...

Beneath all, that color of Mainz sandstone, the hue of dried blood on dust.

For two places only might that rug be fit, Harry thought. Hung as a tapestry behind the high altar of the cathedral in Mainz. Or in the parlor of a whorehouse for the paralytic and maimed.

But nowhere on its obscene surface a dead mouse, not even a cockroach. Then he understood. It had been the carpet itself that was dying. Slowly, horribly dying behind his *Schrank*.

"Come rack!" he cried aloud. He spent a good deal of time that day alternately muttering "Come rack!" and wondering what "Come rack!" meant, exactly.

Harry pulled the mattress off his bed and slept that night in the kitchen, and he dared not dream.

When the advent of postharvest had been duly celebrated with *Handkäse* afloat in its own liquid putridity, and with the opening of radiator valves; when the purgative effects of *Apfelwoi* had been blunted by Kuchen dough lodged in every valve and ventricle of Harry's heart, Bayern and Netherland; when Harry had entered a barren landscape of the soul, where he sat as upon cold ashes, pinched, bile-shot, baleful-eyed; he penciled this legend and pinned it to a corner of his carpet:

"This rug is UGLY and it wants to DIE!"

He had thought the rug would lose its smell if it were properly aired. So, on a crisp, dry day, in a season when the waning daylight filled him with a sense of deprivation, he hung his carpet out his bedroom window, and beat it until the elderly gentleman on the floor below began insinuatingly to cough like a tubercular. Then Harry pulled the window down with the rug half-in and half-out. The stiff mid-autumn breeze rippled and snapped the outside half of the carpet like the flag of the grandest floating whorehouse on the River Styx. He rotated the rug until it was all thoroughly aired.

The airing did revive the rug somewhat. Even the funereal colors seemed to brighten. But within a few hours after he had spread it on the floor again, it began once more to smell, and to die.

Small white flakes appeared on the rug nap. He thought at first they must be moth eggs, but when he swept them away, more flakes shortly took their place. The hideous creature was snowing out the hidden crystals of its life.

And, seeing that his rug wept tears of ugly, bitter, unloved old age, Harry's heart toward it was transformed. He no longer thought of the maddening tint as the color of dried blood on dust. He saw now in his rug the color and design of decaying, demented womanhood.

For womanhood does not simply fade. Unfulfilled, dying, its last flower is a wild and lurid violet, its tears bitter crystals to which maidens' tears are as sweet rain. Its breath is the breath of old whores' graves.

And it came to pass that Harry loved his ugly rug.

He bought rug shampoo and bathed and scrubbed and scoured the nap. It took out some of the color that the airing had restored. But the crystals stopped forming, and never formed again.

Long and long he gazed at his strange, ancient new love, wondering what else she might like.

"Violets," his rug answered in a querulous, old maid's voice. "Bring me violets."

Harry had the violets delivered. "The key is taped under the mailbox lid," he told the florist's clerk. "It's a surprise, you see."

~ * ~

Once, in a season that for a long while would grow more pinched and discontent, Harry's heart toward his carpet was transformed.

Once, in the advent of postharvest, when each bearer of the perfect fur lining for flight boots limped trembling through silver stubble, when the ventricles of hearts and radiators had been duly opened and purged of all detritus, Harry gave his rug violets.

Once when, evening and morning, the pale sun slid along a lower sky the hue of Mainz sandstone, like a wafer sliding on the tongue of a dying invalid, Harry watched his ugly rug bloom.

Haltingly, tremblingly, she put forth her first, her dying blossom. In chisel-dust sandstone twilight, the nap glowed with a haunted ardor. Her breath was the violet breath of an old dame with a lover twenty years her junior.

With tenderness and sweet anticipation, Harry waited for his rug to die.

He wrote his mother, promising to fly home for Christmas. One afternoon he knocked on Frau Link's door. Her eyes were glazed and red, her eyelids puffed, her mouth sullen and tired. But she brightened up when she saw it was Harry.

"Ah, Herr Waters! *Ich hab' einen Kaffeekuchen gemacht!*"

"*Und ich,*" said the graying swain, producing from behind his back a tissue-wrapped bouquet. "*Ich hab' etwas Violetten gebracht!*"

~ * ~

But his rug did not die. It no longer wanted to die. It had something to live for. And that was what it was going to do: live. With all his horror returning, Harry saw that his rug would certainly not die—and, worse, that what it wanted to live for was him. Come rack!

When the violets had withered, he did not buy more. It didn't matter. The single gift and thought, to one deprived of all such, was enough to sustain his carpet. The odor of violets hung upon it like the warm aura of sleep upon a girl at breakfast.

He deprived it of his company. That was all right. Secure in its delusion of love, it welcomed him back each time with a deeper, warmer glow.

He (accidentally) dropped a glowing ash from his cigar onto one of her mausoleum cabbageleaf designs. The healthy, springy nap held the ash away from her body, and only the tips of the strands were singed.

Fleetingly he thought of dousing her with acid. But the mental image of his old, obscene carpet smiling her forgiveness through her scars brought cold sweat from his pores.

One evening, in a season that could not get much colder, and that would kill off a few invalids and sick lovers before it got warmer, Harry, sitting at his desk, felt the rug nap stir and tingle beneath his socked feet. The only light in the room came from his small desk lamp. Looking behind him at the shadowed carpet, he imagined he saw her nightshade vines coiling upward. She was trying to draw him down into her eternal, poisonous embrace.

Seizing his head in his hands, he rushed into the kitchen, shouting, "*Ich wurde verruckt!*"

Willing himself calm as he had learned to do in his days as a combat pilot, Harry went back into his bedroom and switched on the ceiling light. He rolled up the carpet and dragged it down to his car. The night was iron cold, breathlessly cold. He crammed the rug into the trunk and drove to the air base. "Where are you taking me, my love? Where are we going, my love, so late, together? Ah, together! Where, my love? Where, my love, love, love?"

When he got on the autobahn, he drove very fast, all the while twirling with his thumb a little gold ring on his pinkie.

He plied the Spaniard incinerator attendant with Henninger beer. Harry wanted to finish this himself, alone with her. He knew how to set the draft, to bring up the blaze, from his post-pilot period, when he had supervised classified-burn details.

The unfurled carpet made a smothery whump when it landed on the pile of half-burned rubbish in the bottom of that huge iron cylinder. For a while, to Harry, gazing down through the incinerator door, it seemed the rug had actually smothered the fire. Then steam began to spew from beneath the edges. Then the carpet itself began to steam.

The lurid design lit up with a burst of frantic passion. At last she understood. Harry felt his eyebrows start to scorch and curl. The flames ate through the mat slowly and evenly, until only that hellish design seemed to dance on the surface of the fire itself. Properly displayed at last. In the proper parlor.

None but Harry knew her dying fury. A sputtering howl rose from the carpet, as moisture, trapped in the fabric, boiled. A glaring geranium, black and sandstone red, broke off and whirled upward. An instant before it would have flown out into his face, Harry threw the triple-plate door to. He heard the disembodied bloom flap and sizzle against the door. He rubbed his hand across his stinging forehead. His eyebrows came off in ash streaks on his palm.

~ * ~

Harry cleaned and oiled and waxed his bedroom floor. When Frau Link brought up a generous square of pre-Christmas sugar cake, he thanked her, broke off a piece, crumbled it in his fingers, and told her, sorry, but it was too dry and brittle for him. He wrote his mother that he couldn't afford to come home this winter after all. But next summer, for sure.

Dawn Call

Suddenly I'm awake, waiting, I don't know why. Something's pent behind the brittle lip of the desert night. Then it starts. In the 3 a.m. stillness, it sounds like a baritone tomcat tuning up. "*Allaa-hu akhbar!*" Christ, and that's just the first call. It'd be another hour before I could get back to sleep. "*Allaa-hu akhbar!*"

I lie on the turned-down sheet with the dry, prickling coolness running over my skin, while the pale shimmer about the limbs of the dream tree fades in my head. Dogwood? Pear? And why a tree, anyhow? Well, it's spring, after all. It just shows your dream clock is ticking on, even here.

"*Ashadu allaa ilaha illa allah!*" What was it that's different about dawn call? Something about Allah being sweeter than sleep. Like hell He is. Like hell He's sweeter than those blossoms.

All right, You're great. But like hell You deserve being told so five times a day. Especially not now, in the dusty Riyadh spring, with the heat coming back and Steen a year dead come Palm Sunday. With Evelyn in her attic back in Charlottesville now, doping herself against Palm Sunday with iced burgundy and needlepoint and Donne. Evelyn, who would have pulled him out of it, if only she'd been there when you came to slip the blindfold on him. "*Ashadu anna Mohamadan rasuul ullah!*"

I swing out of bed and shuffle to the john and piss in the cat hole. I stand swaying in the piss reek, piss spattering my feet, while the prayer call's harsh dying fall echoes in the ventilation shaft. I stare at the mortar stains on the unfinished wall above the tile, and suddenly I see again the tree, with the pale cloud upon its branches and the shadowy shape pierced by its roots. Mitsuko, that's it. Mitsuko and that little orchard behind the serpentine wall where we went in the rain. Mitsuko and her cherry trees and corpses.

Damn this desert. Damn this empty camel-walk where love can come on you just as quick as God or heatstroke. I pull the flush chain and step to the sink and slop water onto my feet.

From out on Al Khazzan, I hear a metallic crumpling sound. At first I think the transformer at the corner must have blown again. Then I hear jabbering and the slam of a car door, and I shake my head and chuckle.

I towel my hands, shuffle back to my room and pull the folded newspapers out from under a balcony storm door, where I'd stuffed them to block the dust. I stick my head out. Down three stories and up the alley at the median crossover, a silver Mercedes is nuzzled into the side of a cab. A rangy Arab in a cream-white thobe and headcloth stands in the street yelling and lifting his arms like he's calling God to witness. The taxi driver sits with his hands on the wheel. In the light from a street lamp, his eye whites gleam like knobs of bone.

"Nice work, cowboy," I mutter. "Three-thirty a.m. on an empty street and you smack a cab."

What are you doing dogged up like that at this hour, cowboy? Slipping through some princess's bedroom window? Or just Khurais cruising? If it's just that, cowboy, it'll be the most expensive shot of Somalian poontang you ever got.

A breeze brushes my cheek. I sniff it, the way I'd sniff the March breeze at home, ready to sort out the smells of early spring. At home there'd be that wild onion smell, and the smell of earthworms churning the sod—an odor like olive oil worked into the pocket of a baseball glove. And maybe a skunk somewhere. No smell of blossoms yet. Not until after Palm Sunday, when the tree roots have feasted on their corpses. If Evelyn sticks her head out her window before dawn, she'll smell the earth telling her: Palm Sunday, Palm Sunday in two weeks.

I fill my lungs, but there's no smell, just the prickling of dust grains in my nostrils. That's one thing you can say for this desert. The only thing you can smell out here is God. And He smells just like nothing at all.

I shut the storm door and stuff the newspapers back under it. I pull on a jock, knee wrap, my Vietnam fatigues. Keep anything long enough, the day'll come when you need that, and nothing else will do. Keep your Nam fatigues ... someday you'll end up where they yell and throw rocks at you if you run bare-legged. Keep running before dawn ... someday you'll end up where God slaps you awake at 3:30 a.m. to remind you how *akhbar* He is.

If Steen could've lived long enough to find good uses for all the pieces of himself that he hated.

I go out in the dark corridor, pull the door to and drop the key clasp in a cartridge pocket of my fatigue pants. I run down the stairwell. Outside the foyer there's a cop car with two whirling blue lights on top. The cop and the big Arab are standing in the street. The Arab slaps the back of one hand into the palm of the other and jabbers, trying to brazen it out. The taxi driver's still in his car. He's little, dark, weasel-faced, with a scraggly goatee and a dirty white thobe and skull cap. His eyes roll sideways like a scared pony's. There's some fetish junk and a head rope hanging from his rear-view mirror. I jog up past the wreck.

"Aaaay!"

"Oh, shit," I say, thinking it's the cop. But when I turn back, it's the big Arab who's got his arm thrust toward me with the palm up. He lifts his hand and swivels it once, like he's unscrewing an upside-down jar lid above his head. The little cop's eyes beneath the brim of his skull cap look as timid as a kid's.

Like A Wary Blessing

The Arab lifts his hand higher and gives it another twist. What's that supposed to mean? Screw you? Unscrew you? As he moves, a satin sheen runs along his thobe like flame running on an oil slick. He's got thin gold taps on the pointed toes of his shoes. There's a big, mean sneer on his face, and out of it comes a sound like a steam valve opening: "hSSssshh." I point at the cop, then I jerk my thumb at my chest.

"You want me for something?" I ask the cop. "There something in the Sharia against double-tied shoelaces?"

The cop grins shyly. A one-stripe chevron, held on with a pin, dangles from his near sleeve. I feel the vein in my right temple start to throb.

"You can fuck off, Abdulmohsen!" I yell at the Arab. Then I catch myself. I always let them get me. I roar at them like Steen would have done. But Christ, it's nice sometimes to see the fight go out of them when they see you mean business.

This one doesn't flinch, though. His sneer stays put, and he lowers his hand with all five fingers pointing up and spread. It's such a fine, controlled insult that for a moment I just stand there admiring it. He's six feet tall at least, and rangy. First generation off the desert, I'd say. Maybe one of the al-Kahtanis, with plenty of oil money coming in off tribal land. Pure Arab. Funny how they take so much pride in that. But city life leaves them nothing to do with all their purity and pride and money but drive their Mercedes down empty streets past midnight and maybe smack a cab.

The little cop looks like he wants to scatter in four directions at once. I flip the Arab a salute.

"Till we meet again, cowboy," I say. "Better hurry home if you want to catch dawn prayer."

I turn away, but before I can start to run, a bitter tiredness sweeps me. At sunset there was a horned moon over the big, camel-colored new mosque down the street, and the workmen from the sewer project, shrunken-looking in their grimy garments, had straggled past under the stars. Now the sky's a dust-hazed black, brightened only by the rows of aircraft warning lights down by Wazir. There's nothing on the street except two big pneumatic shovels with their many-jointed necks craned and their scoops buried in a trench that runs up one lane from the Mecca Road flyover.

Why in hell do you want to go down there? You're 33 years old and you've got a varicose vein in your head. You've got a mean Arab behind you and the four a.m. emptiness of God in front.

And you're tired, damn it, you're tired. You can go back in and shower, and by then the second call will be done. You can go to bed and maybe catch two more hours. Why do you need to head down that street? It'd be like running down the black muzzle Steen took between his teeth.

Yes, and why after Steen blew himself away did you come out here to the hellhole of the planet, when you could have scuttled back into newspaper work? Just because you thought you'd find Him out here somewhere? Well, some folks just naturally have to go around the elbow. If all you wanted was Him, you didn't need to log 10,000 miles to a place where a tomcat chorus yowls His name every five hours. All you needed was a three-foot shotgun barrel, like Steen.

No, it's not Him you're after. Not except sometimes at four a.m., when He's the only show in town. The rest of the time He's just part of the scenery, just something to stuff the sky with.

What pulled you here is the bucks you need to log that other 10,000 miles, to Yokohama, to take Mitsuko away from that baggy-pantsed old dreamer, so hopped up on Lee's Lieutenants he'd send his daughter to Charlottesville for her junior year. Anything else? Well, the chance to splice two fucked-up, cut-short careers, Air Force and grad school, by teaching English to Saudi flight crews. But that's all. If He wants to think there was something more, let Him. If you hear folks hollering your name as often as He does, you're likely to think a lot of fool things.

I lift my eyes and see the faint metallic gleam of the two crescents atop the mosque's towers. And once more the cherry tree hovers before me with blossoms like a luminous mist.

I start to jog. The vein in my temple feels like something live sewn into the flesh, twitching, but that'll pass. Possible precursor to an aneurysm, the doc said. Plus side, probably not. Other plus side, brain aneurysm is a quick way to go—about as quick as kneeling in Dira Square to take a well-sharpened sword in the neck.

The mosque floats past like a silent ship. Beyond the flyover, I can make out the low, lumpy silhouette of the old city. I think of the black lava spires beneath us that night on Oshima, when the wind on the cliffside road to Motomachi cut at us and drove us back. But beyond the frozen lava there'd been the heaving sea. Beyond the old city's crenelated mud walls and squat, pustule-shaped minarets there's nothing but the starless desert night.

The pinched nerve in my left shoulder stabs me, and I shorten my arm swing. A cat scrambles out of a yellow steel garbage bin onto the sidewalk ahead of me. It crouches, swaying tensely, trying to decide which way to scoot. Then it darts into an alley.

I try to think of the cat, of its vagrant and furtive life, but I can't. On weekend evenings, when I run along the back streets near the television station, it'd be easy. The little Arab boys would leave their street-soccer games and run beside me, laughing and clapping. There'd be little girls in pigtails and dirty frilled dresses standing huge-eyed in the doorways, and bearded old men in gold-trimmed capes hobbling toward the mosques, and the bright scent of green coffee flavored with cardamom. The tall yellow Saluki hounds would gaze out from the courtyards and wag their curled tails stiffly when a child scampered by. Outside the TV station, the guards with their checkered headcloths drawn across their mouths and their rifle butts by their boot heels would turn silently, eyeing me as I passed. The garbage bins would swarm with cats. And I would feel every life brush mine. Even the cats'. Even the lives of lop-eared Nejd sheep, shaggy as Afghan hounds, huddling in the shantytown the squatters knocked together in that rubble field off Mecca Road.

But at four a.m., the cat and I cross paths like meteorites in the emptiness of God.

I run beneath the flyover, past the changing stoplight. Ahead of me the old city looms up. I cut right down an alley, then quickly left to run parallel to Khazzan. Crooked wooden drains sprout like thorns from the walls above me. A bulb burns behind a barred second-floor window. Across the glass moves the shadow of a man shaking water from his hands. Washing up for prayer.

Flopping on a scrap of rug at four a.m. Flopping in the noon heat-shimmer on traffic islands and on the tops of parked buses. That half-blind, splay-footed *mutawa* rapping Abdullah's shop window with his cane, croaking "*Salaat! Salaat!*" The steel shutters rattling down. Sweet hour of prayer. Ali says ten years ago the *mutawaim* would whack truants all the way to the mosque door. Lest Your fourth or fifth daily glut come out one prayer short. The head dangling by a flap of skin from the stretcher's edge, the Arab men spitting into the dark pool of arterial blood on the pavement. That goofy-looking thief's severed hand dangling halfway up the loudspeaker pole with the cord twisted around two fingers.

What Moloch was ever as insatiate as You?

Steen, too, would be up and washed by four. By 4:30 he'd be hunched over that tall black flivver of a typewriter. He'd wrestle with his lamp's rusted gooseneck, light a butt, take one of the fossil stones from the coffee can beside his desk. He'd hold the stone to the light and trace the fossil pattern with a fingertip. Once in a while, he'd peck out a sentence.

And You can be damned sure that none of them was Your name.

I cut left to Khazzan and head down toward Suweylem. I hear a muezzin cough into a mosque microphone. Here it comes, second call. In half a minute they'll all be in full throat.

When I get to the intersection past the park, pandemonium pours over me. It's as if the cries from all the mosques in town converge here. I stand in the street while the racket mounts and mounts. It's like demon laments rolling down all the empty avenues of hell. I peer ahead down Khazzan, hoping for a hint of dawn. But there's nothing, and out of the blackness ahead breaks a fresh Wahhabi snarl.

Steen, buddy. What street corner in hell did you blunder onto before you knew it was there? What demon caterwauling burst over you then? Or did you know you had to go down that black street? And is that why, at church that morning, you wouldn't take a palm leaf?

Like A Wary Blessing

The awful babel fades, and out of it grows a single gentle aria like a flowering tree. "*Ashadu anna Mohamadan rasu-u-u-u-ul ullah!*" Some kid waiting to show off his quarter tones till the old sinecured muezzins are done with their rasping and groaning. If he's got a little honeybunch close by, I'll bet she sleeps through all the rest of it and wakes up when she hears him.

God, it's lovely. How can it be the same thing at all? How can its roots go down into that black, yowling hell? And how can they both be the same?

I run down past the half-fleshed, horseshoe-shaped shell of the Genghini Brothers high-rise. Beneath the footbridge over Wazir Street, in colored spangles that ripple like the scales of a gorgeous sea snake, a gowned child in a garden of red flowers tosses paper into a trash bin. "Help Make Riyadh Clean," the sign says.

I clatter up onto the metal footbridge and look down into the walled grave field. I try to pick out the little stone markers from the jumble of other stones on the bare, humped dust.

Even their kings, they say, they just take out into the desert and shove under the sand somewhere. Believing God will know where to find them, and it's better that other men don't.

Poor buggers. They listened to You. They flopped down five times a day, mumbling Your name with cracked lips. And when they died, all they got was a mouthful of dust and an empty skyful of You.

Beneath every cherry tree a corpse, Mitsuko said. The roots sucking spirit and clear fluid. Well, it doesn't hold the other way around. Lucky the corpse that has its cherry tree. No cherry trees for those who die into You, You howling-empty Bastard.

Yes, the root tendrils coolly laving the heart. Like her lips and tongue when she went down on me. How did she know to do that? Well, nobody had to teach a cherry tree how to love a corpse, either.

How long would it take the cherry roots to get down to Steen through all the dirt we piled on him? Through the lead-lined box? It's kind of hard to feature a cherry tree on that baldhead knob. What a spot for a cemetery. Nobody in that town gets free of his dead. Look out your window and there they are.

Practically pulling the shovels out of the gravediggers' hands. Putting him under the way he'd done for his pop. Yes, his sister Loretta told us he'd want that, but still. A good thing his mother didn't see us. A good thing we didn't tell Evelyn till we got her home.

That old man at the graveside who bayed out his grief like a hound before the women led him away—who was that?

I suddenly realized that, after we marry, I might not be able to see the cherry blossoms for a long while. Of course we can go to Washington, D.C., in the springtime. But there lies a great difference between cherry trees in the U.S. and Japan. I wonder what it could be? Corpse, maybe.

Well, it's not for any lack of good corpses, my love.

And you, poor buggers down there in your walled patch of desert. Dreaming of resurrection, you advertise your whereabouts too well. If God knows where to find you, no cherry tree ever will.

I clatter down the steps on the far side of the bridge. I stretch out a bit on the way down Wazir. My temple's okay now, though I can still feel the thickness there.

Three stubble-jawed day laborers in baggy sailcloth pants, galoshes and headcloths worn turban-wise trudge toward me out of the murk. Must be low on eats. They'll huddle on Smoky Corner for two hours yet before the Dong-Ah and Cansult hiring trucks show up.

The near one glowers at me and hawks a louie at my feet.

You poor broken-backed bastard. Who told you you had a beef with me? Radio Damascus? Some shithead of an *alam*?

I turn, meaning to yell at him. Then I think of how Steen loved those types. Hod carriers, stable boys. Migrants heading up the Valley. Gravediggers. The afternoons I'd found him jawing with some clown in a sopping T-shirt at one of his beloved hot dog counters, passing the mustard squeeze bottle like it was a chalice of brotherhood. He'd have unloaded on that cowboy with the Mercedes, all right. But these guys he'd have loved.

I stare at the back of the filthy smock on the one who spat at me and try to love him. I keep trying for the time it takes to draw a half-dozen breaths of empty desert lung-stuffing. Then I give up and run on.

Seedling on your grave, pal. But how can I make those roots go down?

A little private bus speeds through the Shemaisi Street intersection. A pink dawn flush tinges the black ostrich plume that streams back from its aerial's tip. Up Shemaisi, beyond the arrowhead-shaped crenelations of the Al-Musmak tower and the long white quadrangle of the Friday Mosque, the sky's still a starless soup.

I run up the median toward the mosque. It looks like a ghost-ship prison, with corner minarets instead of guard towers. A hooded old man creeps along the near wall. I wheel off into Dira Square and look up at the clock tower. It's 4:25. Still prayer time. Still time for a quickie.

I jog slowly toward the spot by the clock tower where they chop them. A policeman stands dozing with his back against the door of the Al-Rajhi's exchange up the square. His little machine pistol hangs by a strap from his shoulder. The gun's muzzle dips lower and lower as he falls deeper into his doze.

I stop where they cut them. I peer at the pavement for blood stains, but see nothing but the layer of smudges left by cars and buses. When Mark and I came down here after they'd chopped the Mecca people, the misting rain and traffic had spread the blood until an iridescent film of it covered the whole square this side of the mosque. There was still a good-sized pool of it right here, with grey shreds of hacked flesh in it. The Arabs stood around it, whispering, with their headcloths drawn across their mouths and noses against the reek. There was a man in pure white, with fine, shining, bloodshot eyes, that they all crowded around. He'd beckon them closer still, and then he'd lean forward and draw his headcloth aside and whisper something. Just a word or two, it seemed. And the ones who'd been close enough to hear it would turn aside with the light of it in their faces. Time and again he did that.

He might have been a justice ministry flunky posted there to tell who got cut. Or an *alam* giving a word of blessing. He didn't have the donkey-faced look of an *alam*, though. I'd give a lot to know what that word was.

And the tall, whippet-thin one of the pair we watched get cut, the one who swayed that way—what got whispered to him? Even after they had wrestled him to his knees, his body kept going in those long, undulant swings. Until the executioner bent down and told him something, a word or two, that made him hold still for the sword.

Lean down, Your Emptiness, before dawn prayer's done, and whisper me that word. Whisper me what You whispered to Steen to make him hold still while You cut him.

Whisper to Evelyn what Donne can't. Whisper her the word that will let her turn away in peace.

Don't blare at me, in old men's phlegm-strangled voices, how great You are. Save it for those who got up too late or turned back too soon.

Whisper how the cherry roots can pierce a lead-lined coffin. Whisper how the scent of blossoms can wash the blood reek off Dira Square.

Whisper how we can die into life. Whisper how we can escape ever dying into You.

Whisper, o Sweeter than Sleep. Whisper why, with a little blue viper wriggling on my temple, I chase You down the desert night.

I turn away and shuffle-jog up the square. The dawn gives a pink cast to the mosque's white brick. A fat dawn star swims drunkenly above the crazy jumble of corrugated tin and planks and torn canvas that roofs the old souk. In a few hours, the Sudanese women will come and spread their blankets on the sidewalk and sit among their pans of pistachios and sunflower seeds and candy with their soft, gnarled hands resting in their laps. The little Yemeni porters in faded green skirts and big money belts and high-topped hushpuppies will scurry along the aisles with their ropes and wheelbarrows. Did anybody ever have a bigger money belt and less to put in it than a Yemeni porter? The incense vendors will touch chips of sandalwood to the coals in their braziers, and the clear, heady scent will flood the aisles.

Now the awnings still cover the rusted shutters; the aisles are dark. The cop lifts his head as I pass. Then he shoves himself away from the black cast-iron door and swings his machine pistol's snout toward me.

It's my fatigues. They make the TV station guards nervous, too. Maybe he thinks I'm a Jewish commando, come to piss in the house of prayer.

I flip him a salute before I turn the mosque corner. His hand lifts from his weapon's breech in a faint, palm-down sign, like a wary blessing.

Meet Michael Jennings

Michael Jennings is a North Carolina native and a former newspaper reporter and editor. His service in the Air Force included tours of duty in Vietnam (1969-70) and Germany (1971-73).

He holds an undergraduate degree from the University of North Carolina and a master's degree from the University of Virginia. In 1993, he won a first prize in non-deadline writing from the American Society of Newspaper Editors. He is the author of the novel *Ave Antonina*, published by Wings ePress in February 2020.

Other Works From The Pen Of

Michael Jennings

Ave Antonina - A "schoolmarm in jungle fatigues" flunks out of one war, but his bond with a fellow soldier earns him merit in a different one.

Letter to Our Readers

Enjoy this book?

You can make a difference

As an independent publisher, Wings ePress, Inc. does not have the financial clout of the large New York Publishers. We can't afford large magazine spreads or subway posters to tell people about our quality books.

But, we do have something much more effective and powerful than ads. We have a large base of loyal readers.

Honest Reviews help bring the attention of new readers to our books.

If you enjoyed this book, we would appreciate it if you would spend a few minutes posting a review on the site where you purchased this book or on the Wings ePress, Inc. webpages at: https://wingsepress.com/

Thank You

Visit Our Website

For The Full Inventory
Of Quality Books:

Wings ePress.Inc
https://wingsepress.com/

Quality trade paperbacks and downloads
in multiple formats,
in genres ranging from light romantic comedy
to general fiction and horror.
Wings has something for every reader's taste.
Visit the website, then bookmark it.
We add new titles each month!

Wings ePress Inc.
3000 N. Rock Road
Newton, KS 67114

www.ingramcontent.com/pod-product-compliance
Lightning Source LLC
LaVergne TN
LVHW012102070526
838200LV00074BA/3997